W9-CKI-023

STONE ARCH BOOKS
a capstone imprint

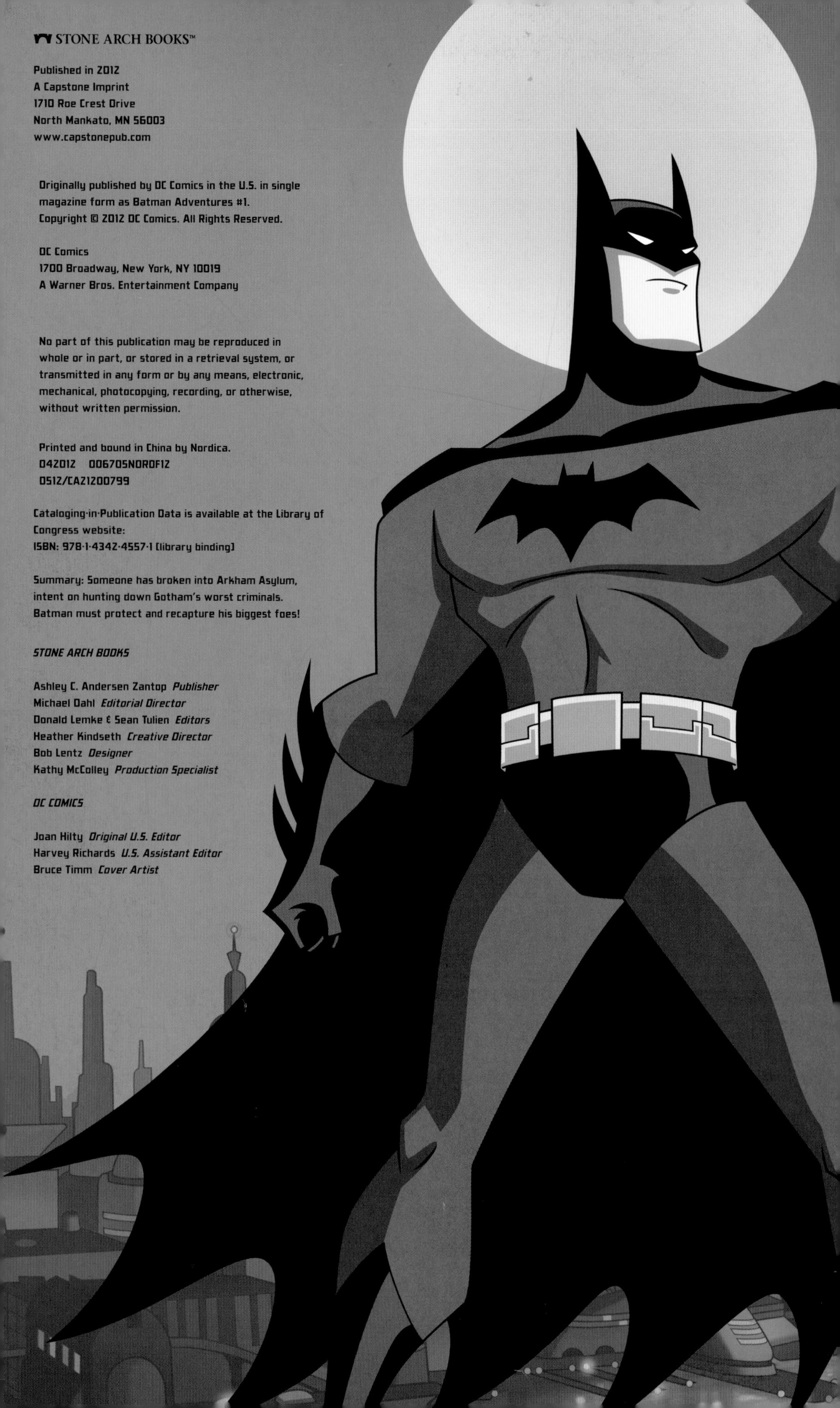

STONE ARCH BOOKS™

Published in 2012
A Capstone Imprint
1710 Roe Crest Drive
North Mankato, MN 56003
www.capstonepub.com

Originally published by DC Comics in the U.S. in single magazine form as Batman Adventures #1.

DC Comics
1700 Broadway, New York, NY 10019
A Warner Bros. Entertainment Company

Printed and bound in China by Nordica.
042012 006705NORDF12
0512/CA21200799

Cataloging-in-Publication Data is available at the Library of Congress website:
ISBN: 978-1-4342-4557-1 (library binding)

Summary: Someone has broken into Arkham Asylum, intent on hunting down Gotham's worst criminals. Batman must protect and recapture his biggest foes!

STONE ARCH BOOKS

Ashley C. Andersen Zantop *Publisher*
Michael Dahl *Editorial Director*
Donald Lemke & Sean Tulien *Editors*
Heather Kindseth *Creative Director*
Bob Lentz *Designer*
Kathy McColley *Production Specialist*

DC COMICS

Joan Hilty *Original U.S. Editor*
Harvey Richards *U.S. Assistant Editor*
Bruce Timm *Cover Artist*

BATMAN ADVENTURES

NO ASYLUM

Ty Templeton & Dan Slott........................writers
Rick Burchett & Ty Templeton .... pencillers
Terry Beatty .... inker
Lee Loughridge.. colorist
Phil Felix ....letterer

Batman created by
Bob Kane

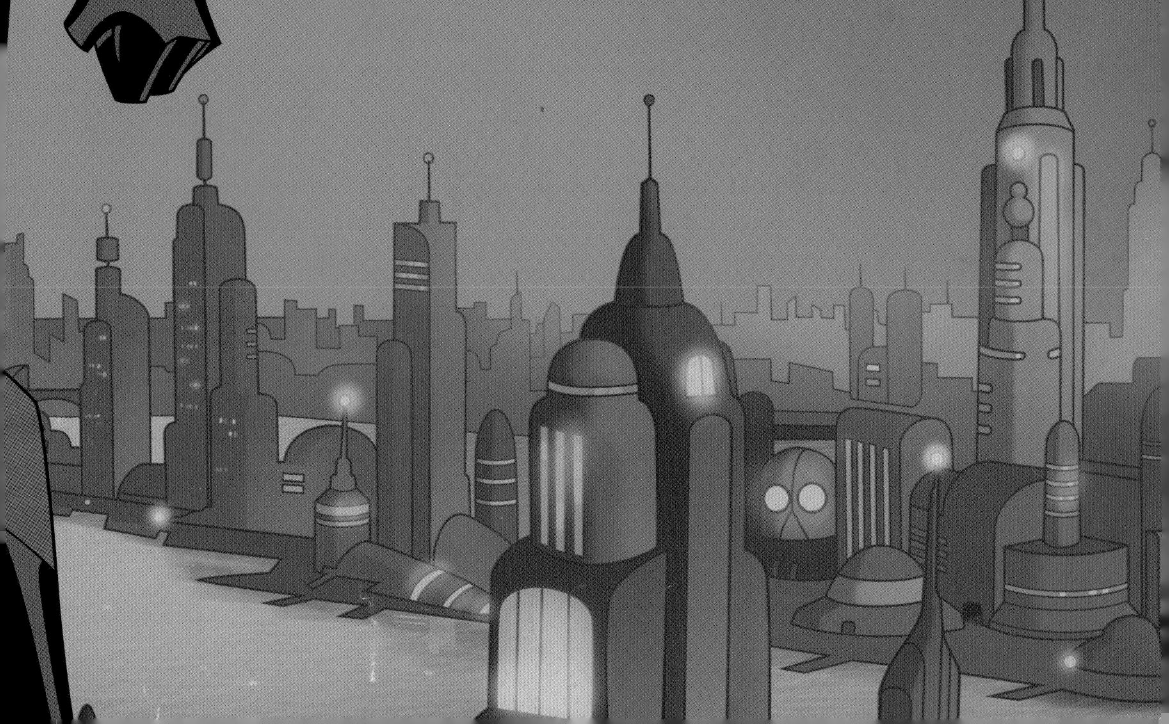

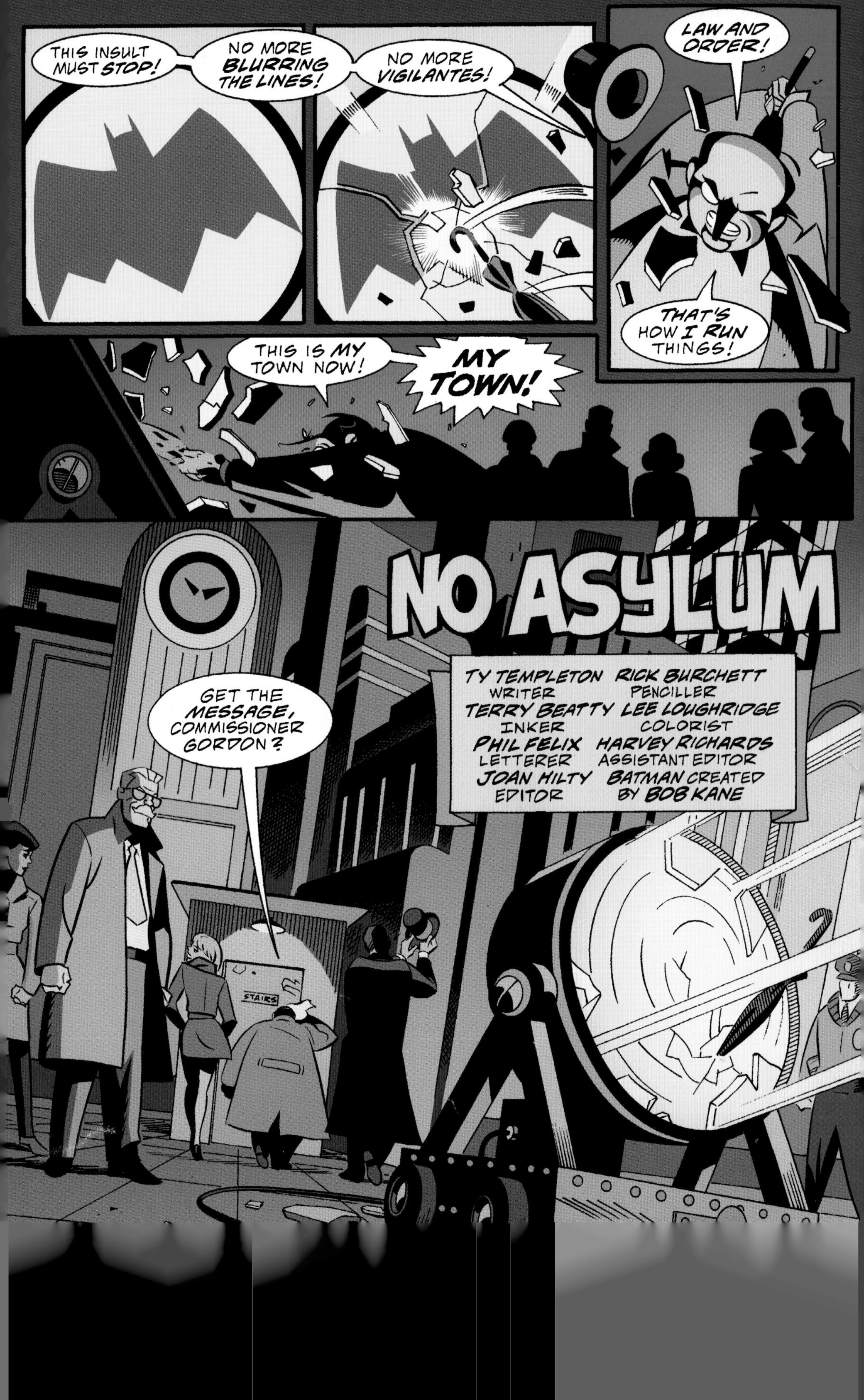

THIS INSULT MUST STOP!
NO MORE BLURRING THE LINES!
NO MORE VIGILANTES!
LAW AND ORDER!
THAT'S HOW I RUN THINGS!
THIS IS MY TOWN NOW!
MY TOWN!
NO ASYLUM
TY TEMPLETON WRITER
RICK BURCHETT PENCILLER
TERRY BEATTY INKER
LEE LOUGHRIDGE COLORIST
PHIL FELIX LETTERER
HARVEY RICHARDS ASSISTANT EDITOR
JOAN HILTY EDITOR
BATMAN CREATED BY BOB KANE
GET THE MESSAGE, COMMISSIONER GORDON?
STAIRS

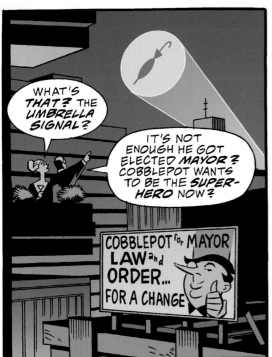

WHAT'S *THAT?* THE UMBRELLA SIGNAL?

IT'S NOT ENOUGH HE GOT ELECTED *MAYOR?* COBBLEPOT WANTS TO BE THE *SUPER-HERO* NOW?

COBBLEPOT for MAYOR
LAW and ORDER...
FOR A CHANGE

COMPUTER,

DIAL COMMISSIONER GORDON'S OFFICE.

HELLO?

LOOKS LIKE PENGUIN IS KEEPING HIS CAMPAIGN PROMISE ABOUT ME...

I'VE GOT A BLACK-AND-WHITE ON MY TAIL.

UNIT *5607.* OFFICER SPERLING, ISN'T IT?

HE'S NOT MUCH OF A DRIVER...

I...

...I DON'T WANT HIM TO GET HURT.

I CAN'T DO ANYTHING ABOUT IT, BATMAN.

OUR *NEW MAYOR* MADE IT CLEAR HE CONSIDERED YOU AN *OUTLAW* ON THE DAY HE WAS SWORN INTO OFFICE.

SCREECH!

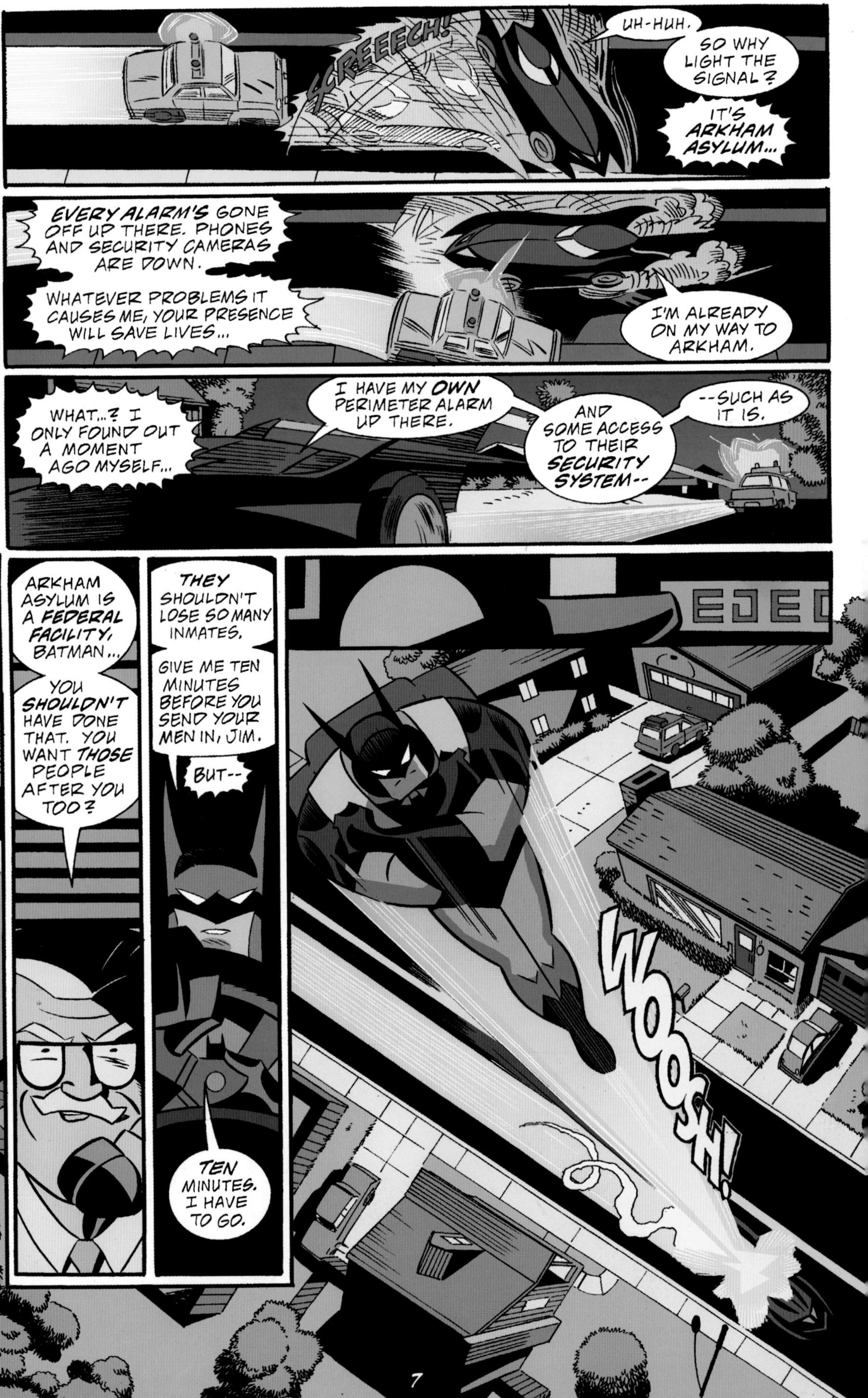
SCREEEECH!
UH-HUH.
SO WHY LIGHT THE SIGNAL?
IT'S ARKHAM ASYLUM...
EVERY ALARM'S GONE OFF UP THERE. PHONES AND SECURITY CAMERAS ARE DOWN.
WHATEVER PROBLEMS IT CAUSES ME, YOUR PRESENCE WILL SAVE LIVES...
I'M ALREADY ON MY WAY TO ARKHAM.
WHAT...? I ONLY FOUND OUT A MOMENT AGO MYSELF...
I HAVE MY OWN PERIMETER ALARM UP THERE.
AND SOME ACCESS TO THEIR SECURITY SYSTEM--
--SUCH AS IT IS.
ARKHAM ASYLUM IS A FEDERAL FACILITY, BATMAN...
YOU SHOULDN'T HAVE DONE THAT. YOU WANT THOSE PEOPLE AFTER YOU TOO?
THEY SHOULDN'T LOSE SO MANY INMATES.
GIVE ME TEN MINUTES BEFORE YOU SEND YOUR MEN IN, JIM.
BUT--
TEN MINUTES. I HAVE TO GO.
WOOSH!

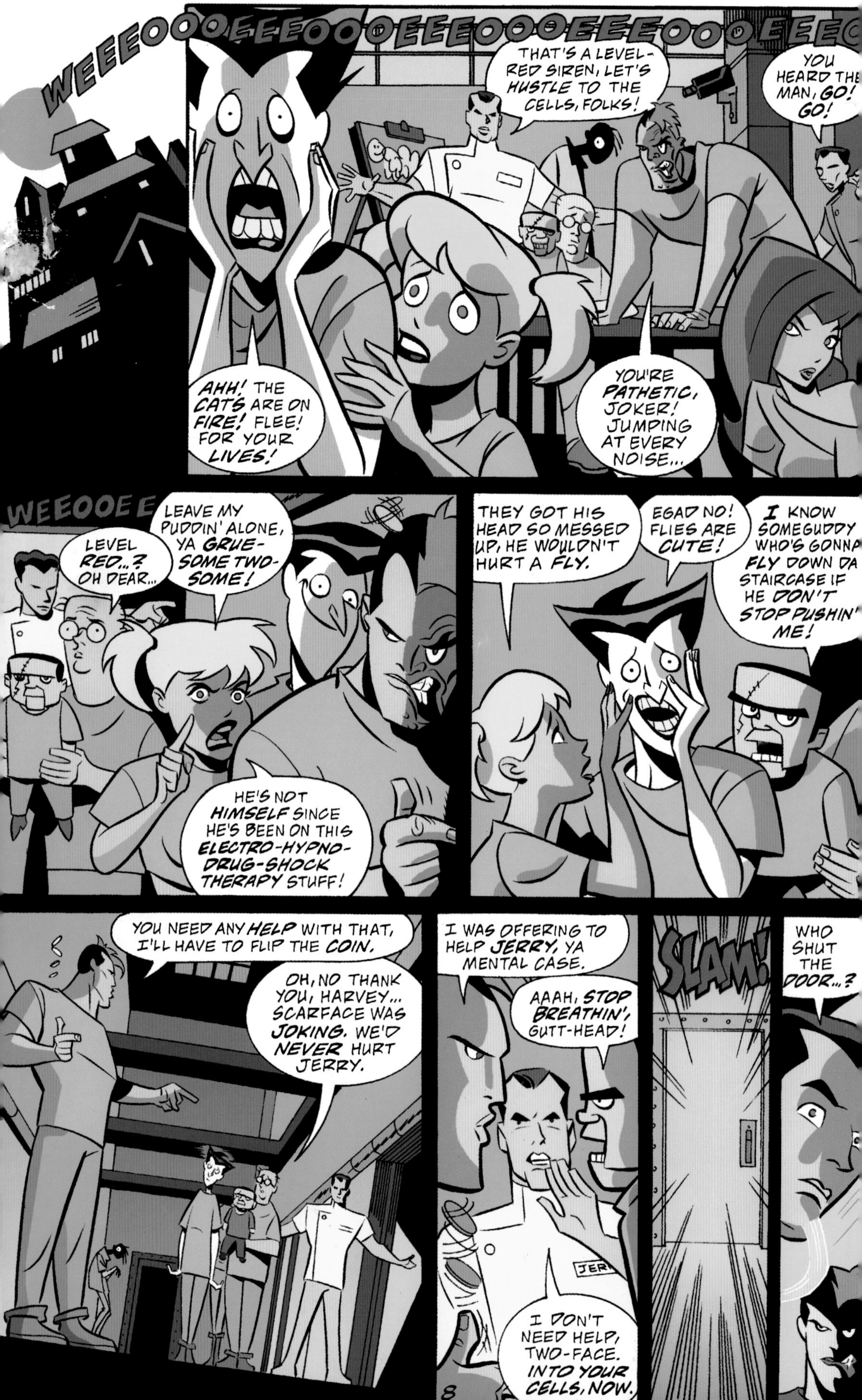
WEEEOOOEEEOOOEEEOOOEEEOOOEEEO
THAT'S A LEVEL-RED SIREN, LET'S HUSTLE TO THE CELLS, FOLKS!
YOU HEARD THE MAN, GO! GO!
AHH! THE CATS ARE ON FIRE! FLEE! FOR YOUR LIVES!
YOU'RE PATHETIC, JOKER! JUMPING AT EVERY NOISE...
WEEOOEE
LEVEL RED...? OH DEAR...
LEAVE MY PUDDIN' ALONE, YA GRUESOME TWOSOME!
HE'S NOT HIMSELF SINCE HE'S BEEN ON THIS ELECTRO-HYPNO-DRUG-SHOCK THERAPY STUFF!
THEY GOT HIS HEAD SO MESSED UP, HE WOULDN'T HURT A FLY.
EGAD NO! FLIES ARE CUTE!
I KNOW SOMEGUDDY WHO'S GONNA FLY DOWN DA STAIRCASE IF HE DON'T STOP PUSHIN' ME!
YOU NEED ANY HELP WITH THAT, I'LL HAVE TO FLIP THE COIN.
OH, NO THANK YOU, HARVEY... SCARFACE WAS JOKING. WE'D NEVER HURT JERRY.
I WAS OFFERING TO HELP JERRY, YA MENTAL CASE.
AAAH, STOP BREATHIN', GUTT-HEAD!
I DON'T NEED HELP, TWO-FACE. INTO YOUR CELLS, NOW.
SLAM!
WHO SHUT THE DOOR...?

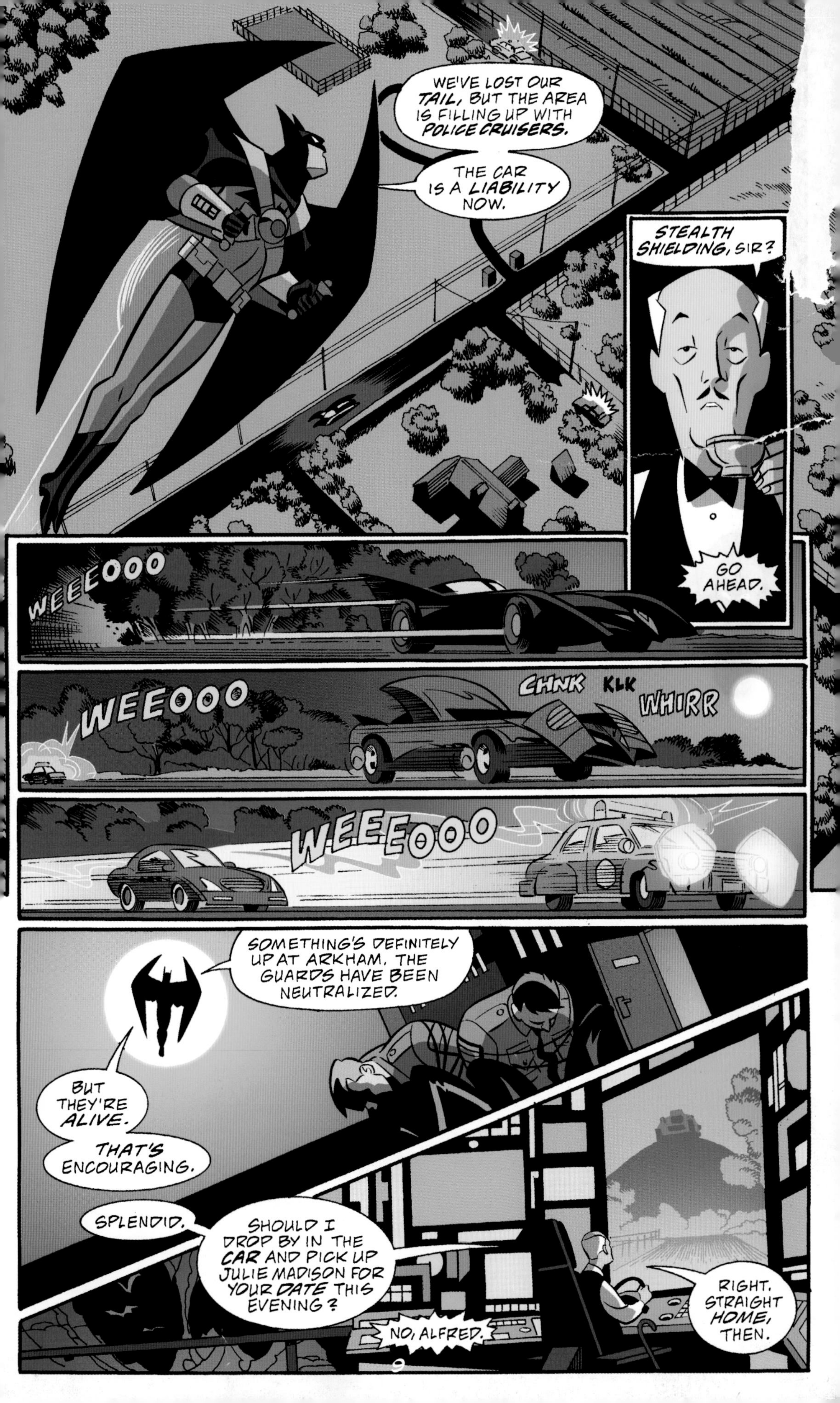
WE'VE LOST OUR TAIL, BUT THE AREA IS FILLING UP WITH POLICE CRUISERS.
THE CAR IS A LIABILITY NOW.
STEALTH SHIELDING, SIR?
GO AHEAD.
WEEEOOO
WEEOOO
CHNK
KLK
WHIRR
WEEEOOO
SOMETHING'S DEFINITELY UP AT ARKHAM. THE GUARDS HAVE BEEN NEUTRALIZED.
BUT THEY'RE ALIVE.
THAT'S ENCOURAGING.
SPLENDID.
SHOULD I DROP BY IN THE CAR AND PICK UP JULIE MADISON FOR YOUR DATE THIS EVENING?
NO, ALFRED.
RIGHT. STRAIGHT HOME, THEN.
9

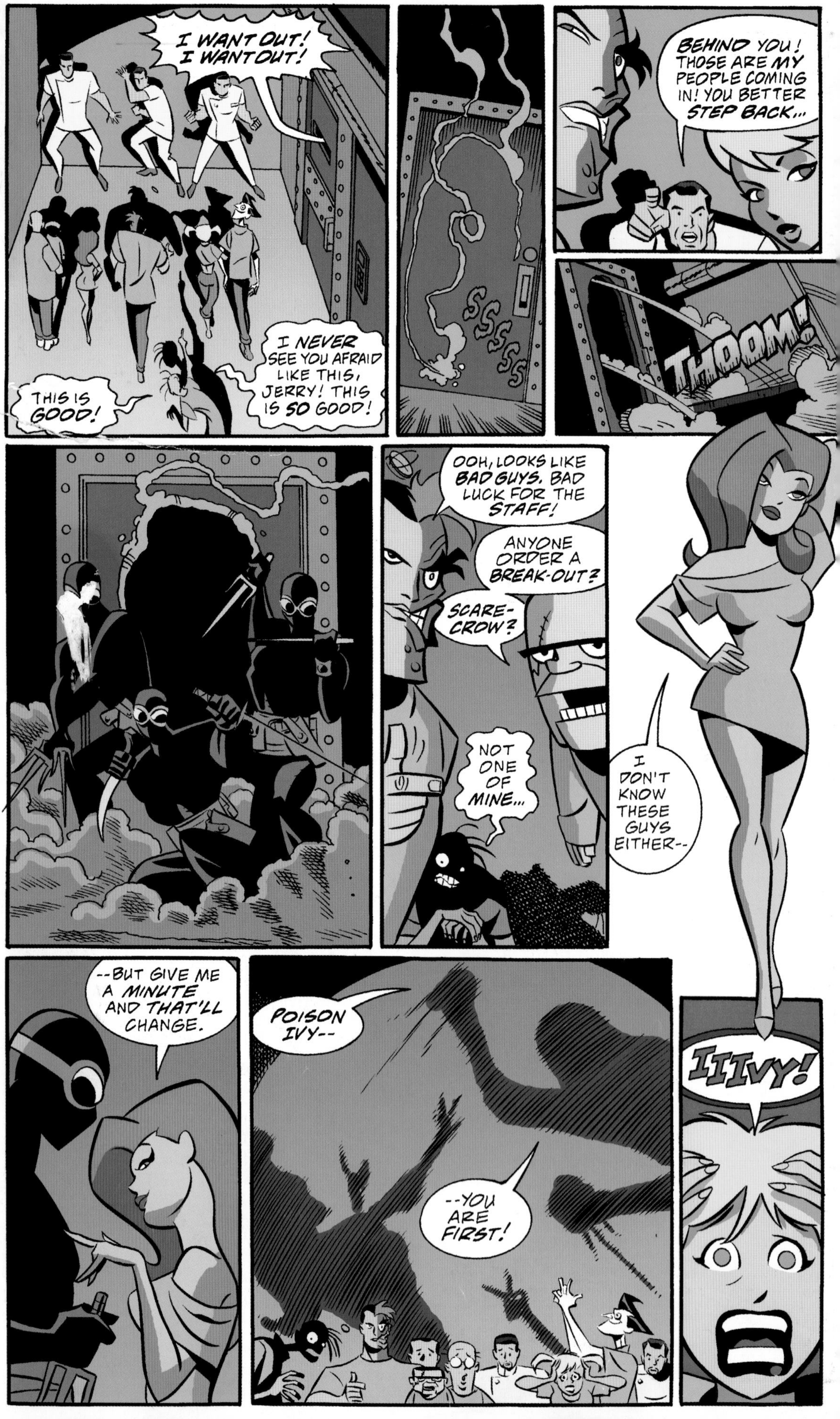

I WANT OUT! I WANT OUT!
I NEVER SEE YOU AFRAID LIKE THIS, JERRY! THIS IS SO GOOD!
THIS IS GOOD!
SSSSS
BEHIND YOU! THOSE ARE MY PEOPLE COMING IN! YOU BETTER STEP BACK...
THOOM!
OOH, LOOKS LIKE BAD GUYS. BAD LUCK FOR THE STAFF!
ANYONE ORDER A BREAK-OUT?
SCARE-CROW?
NOT ONE OF MINE...
I DON'T KNOW THESE GUYS EITHER--
--BUT GIVE ME A MINUTE AND THAT'LL CHANGE.
POISON IVY--
--YOU ARE FIRST!
IIIVY!

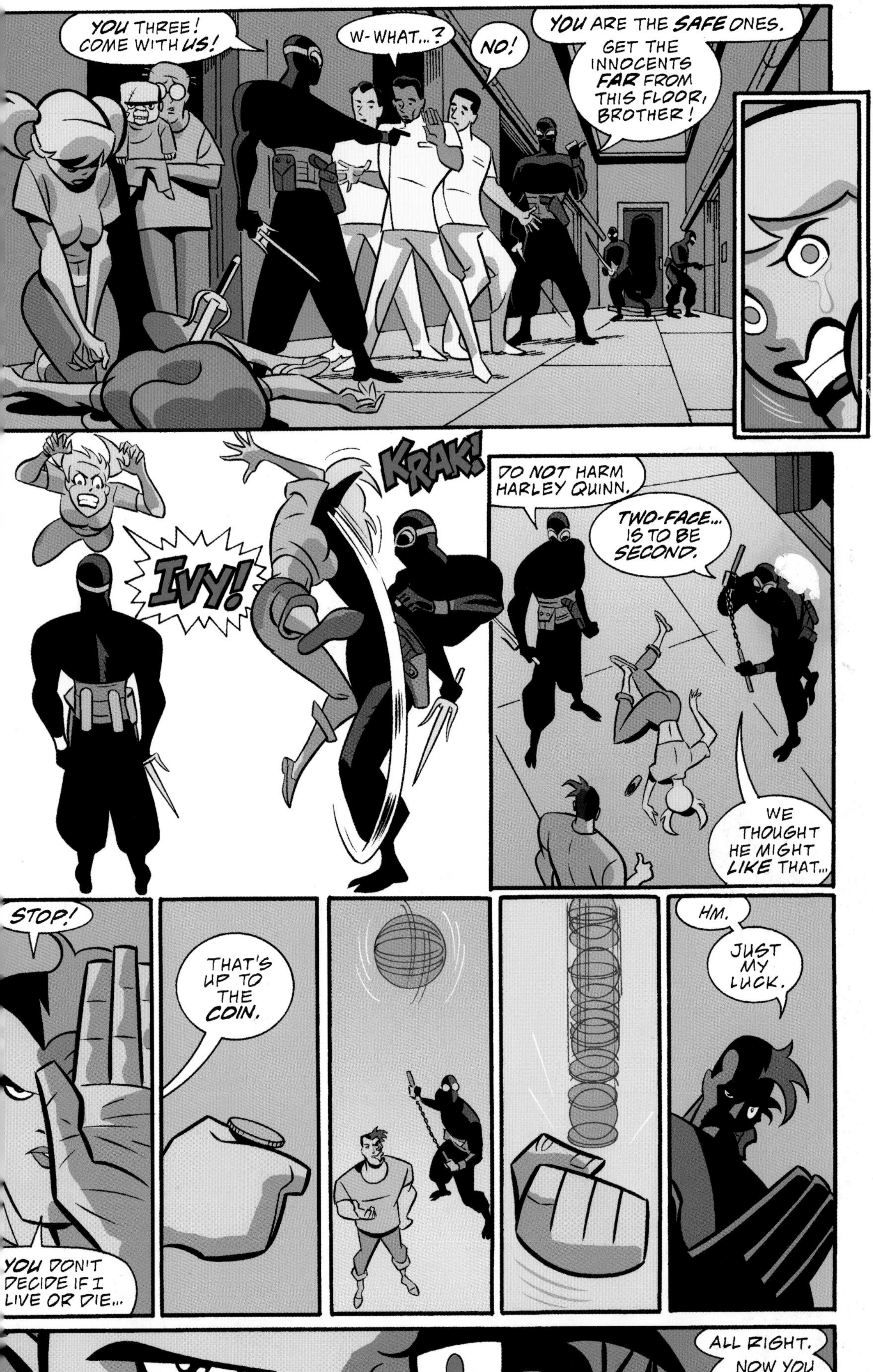
YOU THREE! COME WITH US!
W-WHAT...?
NO!
YOU ARE THE SAFE ONES.
GET THE INNOCENTS FAR FROM THIS FLOOR, BROTHER!
IVY!
KRAK!
DO NOT HARM HARLEY QUINN.
TWO-FACE... IS TO BE SECOND.
WE THOUGHT HE MIGHT LIKE THAT...
STOP!
YOU DON'T DECIDE IF I LIVE OR DIE...
THAT'S UP TO THE COIN.
HM.
JUST MY LUCK.
ALL RIGHT.
NOW YOU CAN COME AT ME.

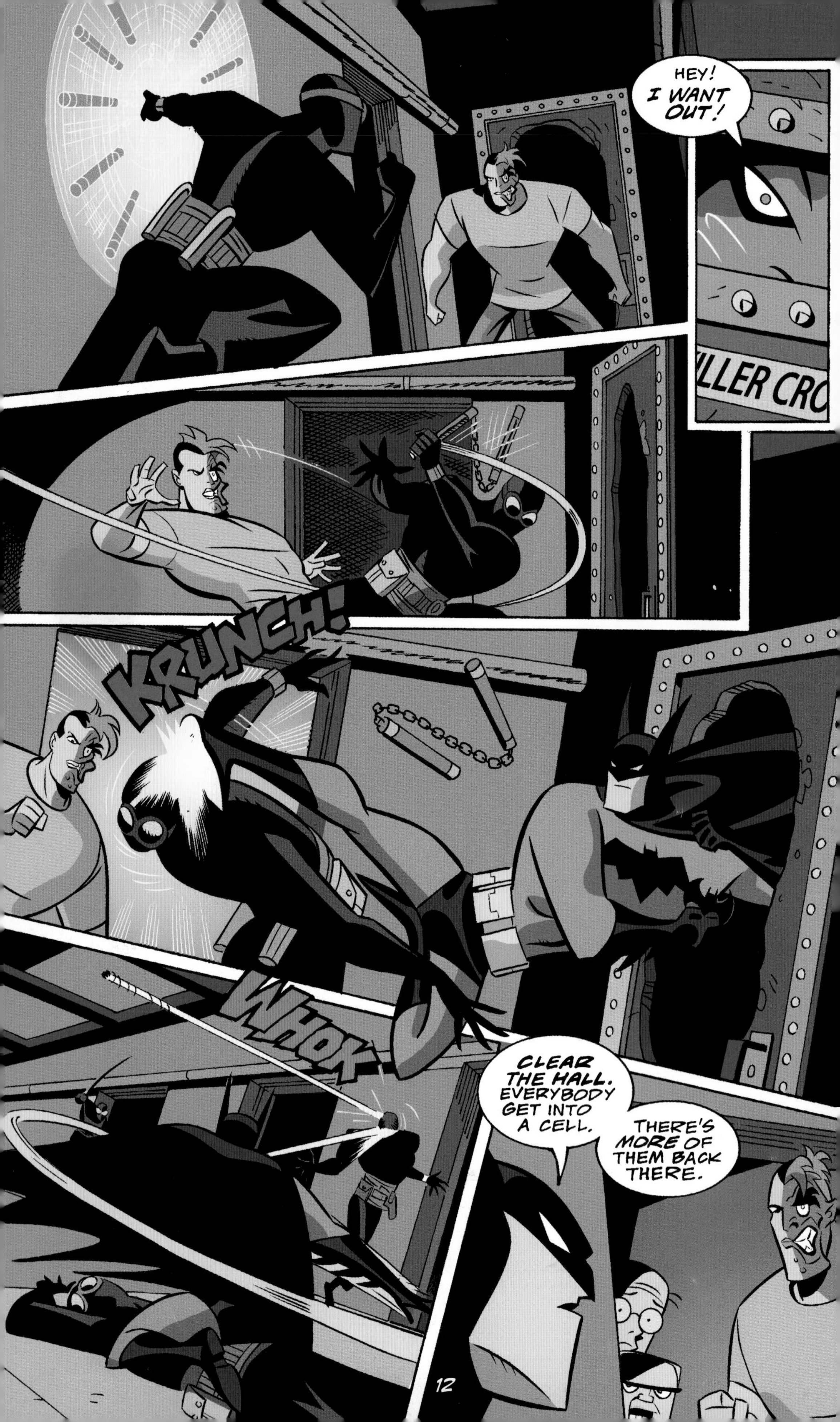
HEY! I WANT OUT!
ILLER CRO
KRUNCH!
WHOK
CLEAR THE HALL. EVERYBODY GET INTO A CELL.
THERE'S MORE OF THEM BACK THERE.

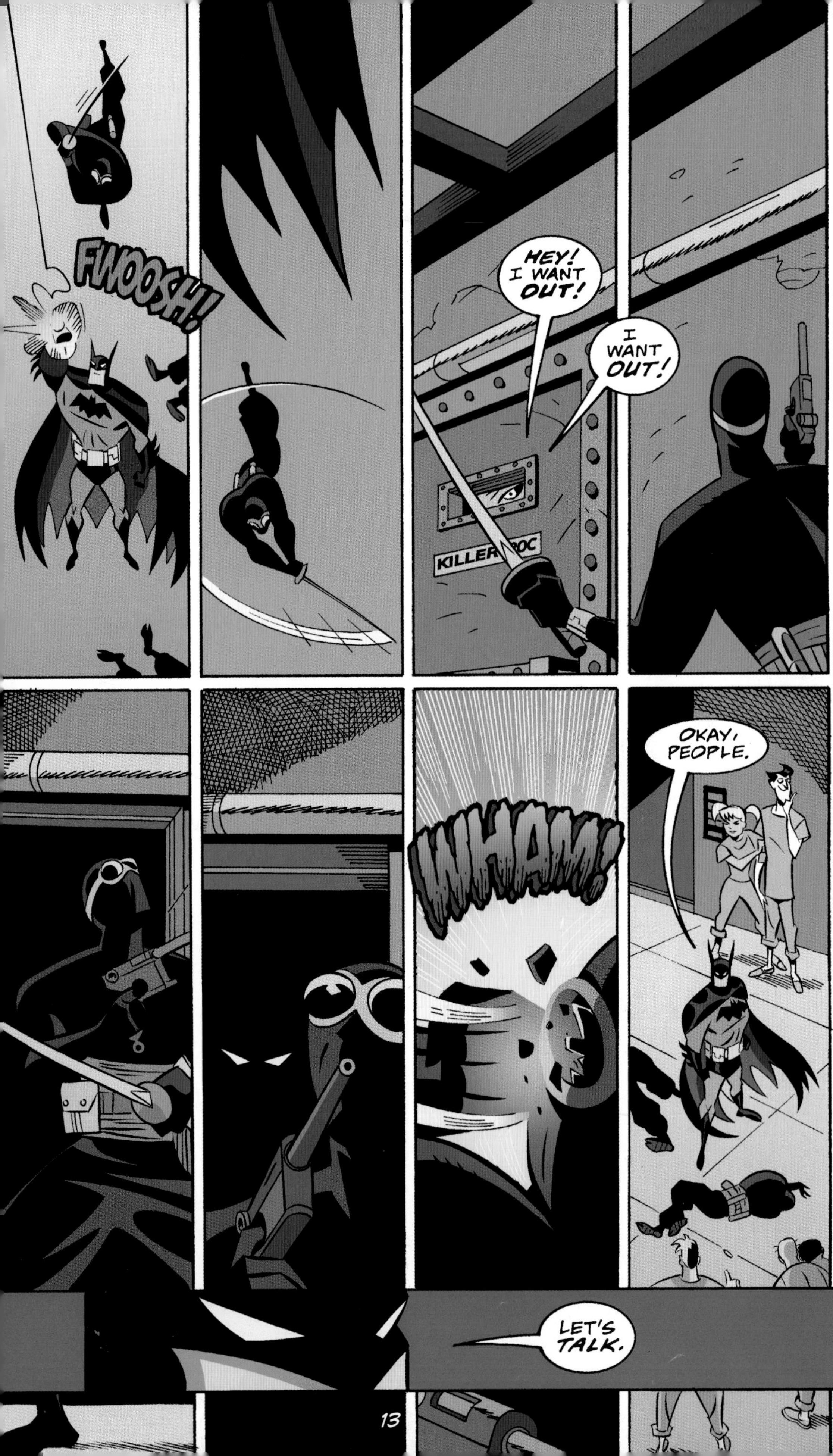

FWOOSH!
HEY! I WANT OUT!
I WANT OUT!
KILLER CROC
WHAM!
OKAY, PEOPLE.
LET'S TALK.

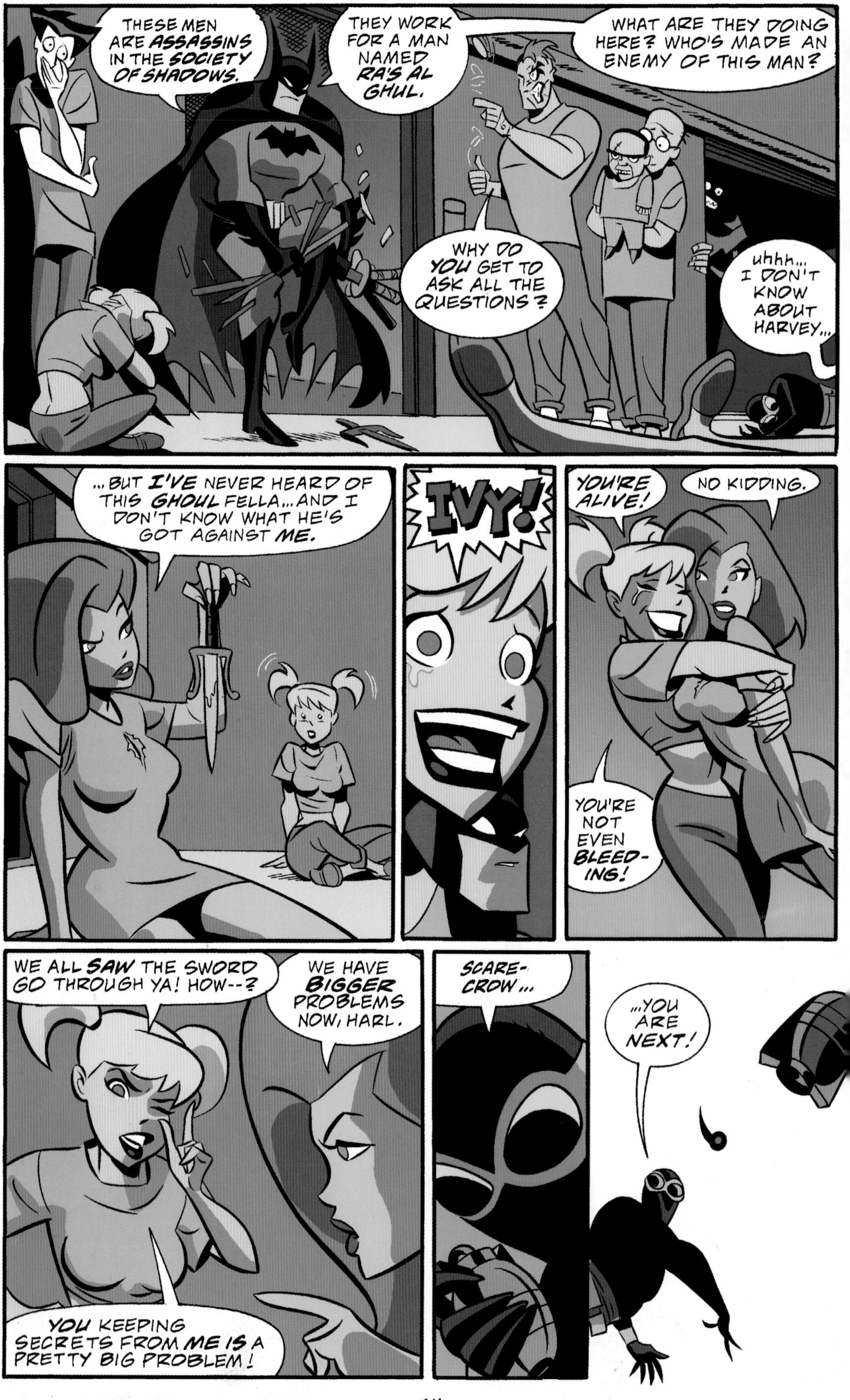
THESE MEN ARE ASSASSINS IN THE SOCIETY OF SHADOWS.
THEY WORK FOR A MAN NAMED RA'S AL GHUL.
WHAT ARE THEY DOING HERE? WHO'S MADE AN ENEMY OF THIS MAN?
WHY DO YOU GET TO ASK ALL THE QUESTIONS?
uhhh... I DON'T KNOW ABOUT HARVEY...
...BUT I'VE NEVER HEARD OF THIS GHOUL FELLA... AND I DON'T KNOW WHAT HE'S GOT AGAINST ME.
IVY!
YOU'RE ALIVE!
NO KIDDING.
YOU'RE NOT EVEN BLEED-ING!
WE ALL SAW THE SWORD GO THROUGH YA! HOW--?
WE HAVE BIGGER PROBLEMS NOW, HARL.
YOU KEEPING SECRETS FROM ME IS A PRETTY BIG PROBLEM!
SCARE-CROW...
...YOU ARE NEXT!

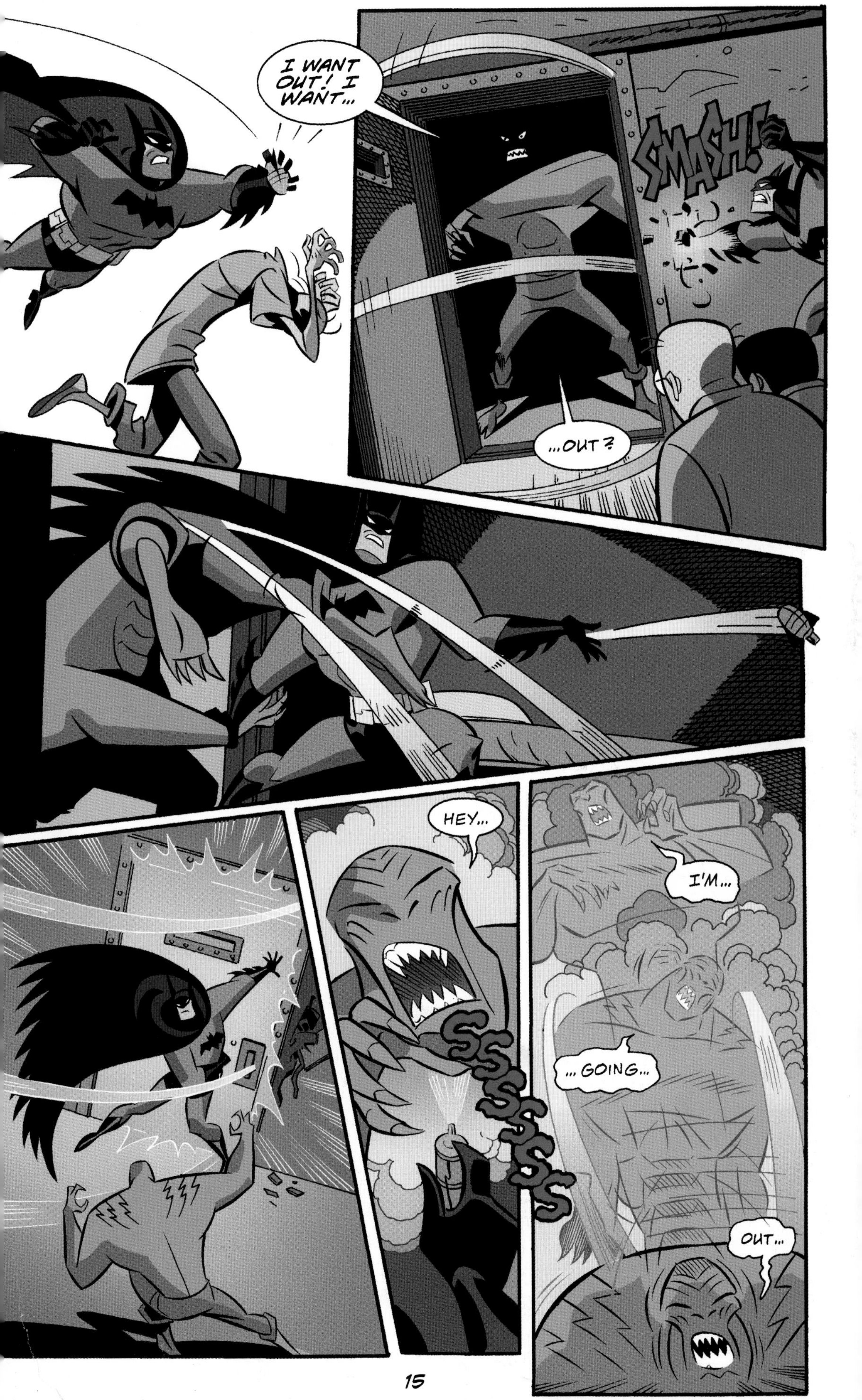
I WANT OUT! I WANT...
SMASH!
...OUT?
HEY...
SSSSSSS
I'M...
...GOING...
OUT...

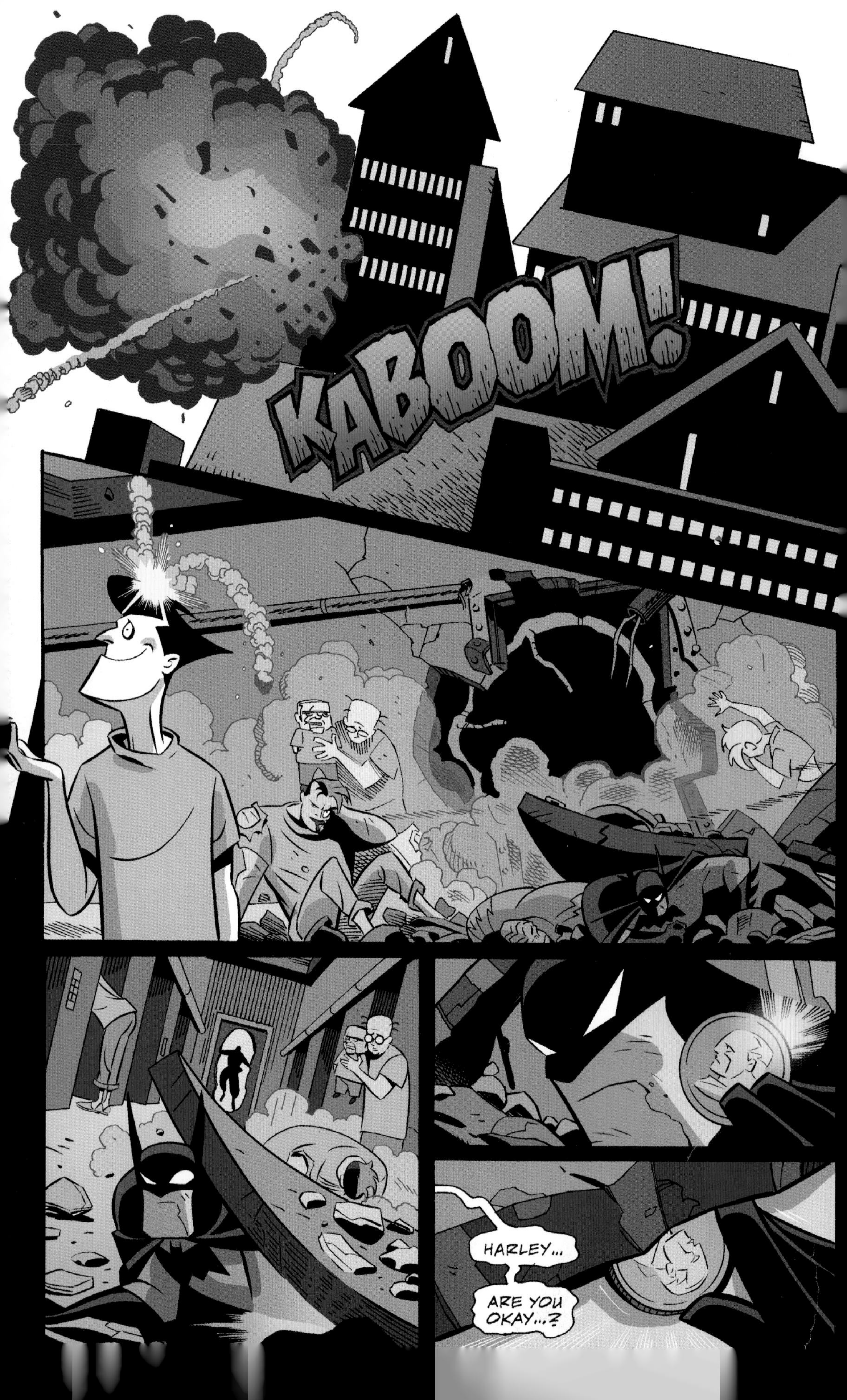
KABOOM!
HARLEY...
ARE YOU OKAY...?

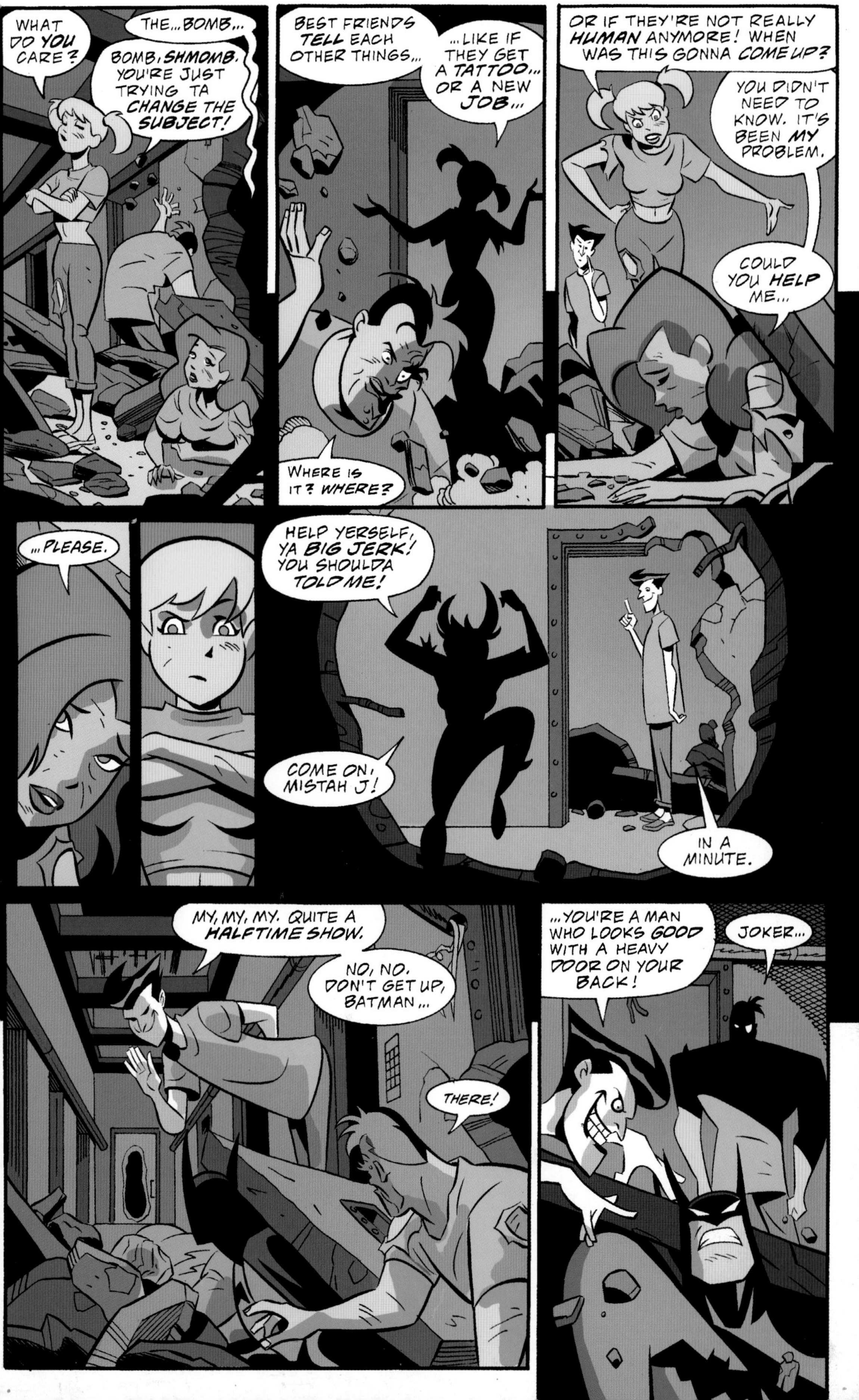
WHAT DO YOU CARE?
THE...BOMB...
BOMB, SHMOMB. YOU'RE JUST TRYING TA CHANGE THE SUBJECT!
BEST FRIENDS TELL EACH OTHER THINGS...
...LIKE IF THEY GET A TATTOO... OR A NEW JOB...
WHERE IS IT? WHERE?
OR IF THEY'RE NOT REALLY HUMAN ANYMORE! WHEN WAS THIS GONNA COME UP?
YOU DIDN'T NEED TO KNOW. IT'S BEEN MY PROBLEM.
COULD YOU HELP ME...
...PLEASE.
HELP YERSELF, YA BIG JERK! YOU SHOULDA TOLD ME!
COME ON, MISTAH J!
IN A MINUTE.
MY, MY, MY. QUITE A HALFTIME SHOW.
NO, NO. DON'T GET UP, BATMAN...
THERE!
...YOU'RE A MAN WHO LOOKS GOOD WITH A HEAVY DOOR ON YOUR BACK!
JOKER...

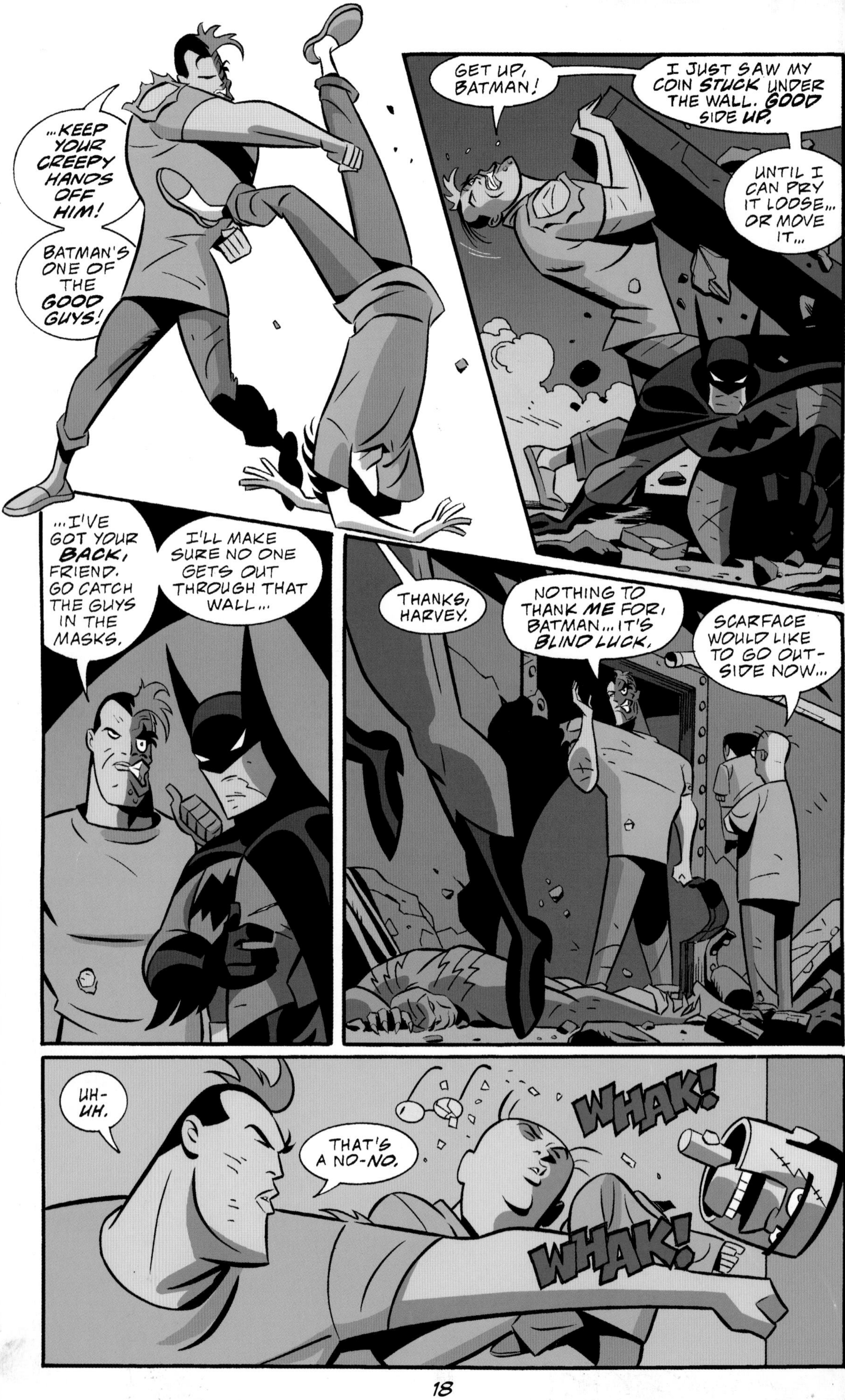

...KEEP YOUR CREEPY HANDS OFF HIM!
BATMAN'S ONE OF THE GOOD GUYS!
GET UP, BATMAN!
I JUST SAW MY COIN STUCK UNDER THE WALL. GOOD SIDE UP.
UNTIL I CAN PRY IT LOOSE... OR MOVE IT...
...I'VE GOT YOUR BACK, FRIEND. GO CATCH THE GUYS IN THE MASKS.
I'LL MAKE SURE NO ONE GETS OUT THROUGH THAT WALL...
THANKS, HARVEY.
NOTHING TO THANK ME FOR, BATMAN... IT'S BLIND LUCK.
SCARFACE WOULD LIKE TO GO OUT-SIDE NOW...
UH-UH.
THAT'S A NO-NO.
WHAK!
WHAK!

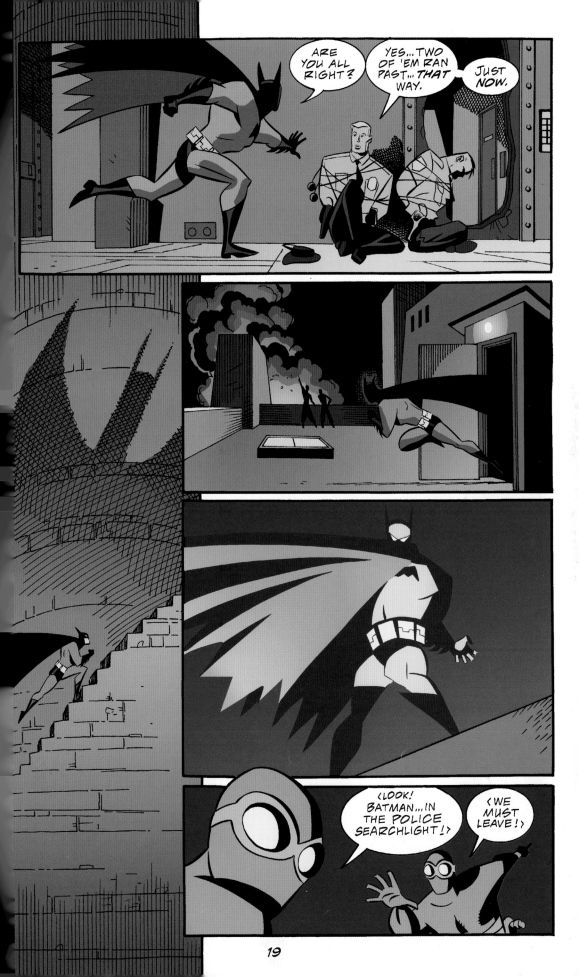

ARE YOU ALL RIGHT?

YES... TWO OF 'EM RAN PAST... *THAT* WAY.

JUST *NOW*.

⟨LOOK! BATMAN... IN THE POLICE SEARCHLIGHT!⟩

⟨WE MUST LEAVE!⟩

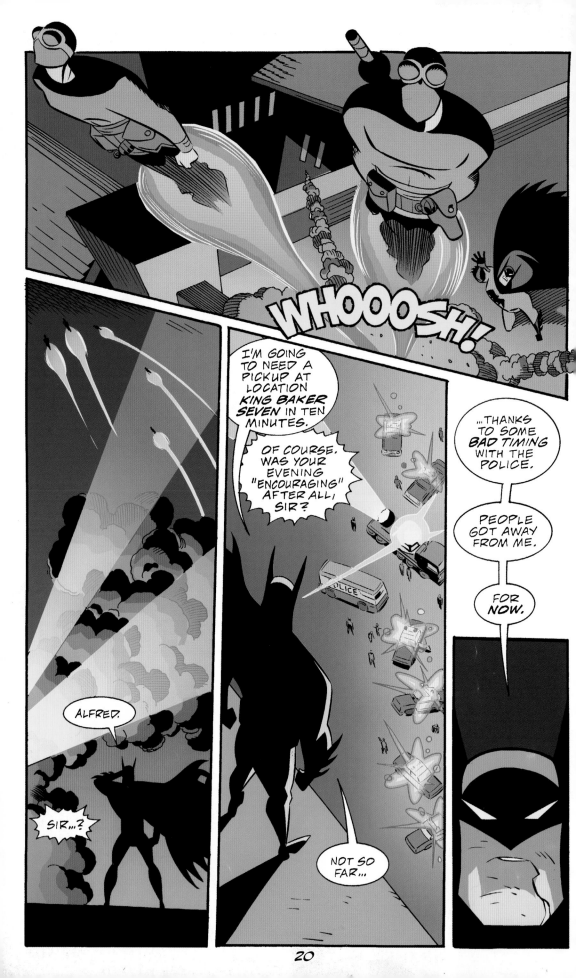

WHOOOSH!

I'M GOING TO NEED A PICKUP AT LOCATION *KING BAKER SEVEN* IN TEN MINUTES.

OF COURSE. WAS YOUR EVENING "ENCOURAGING" AFTER ALL, SIR?

...THANKS TO SOME *BAD TIMING* WITH THE POLICE.

PEOPLE GOT AWAY FROM ME.

FOR *NOW.*

ALFRED.

SIR...?

NOT SO FAR...

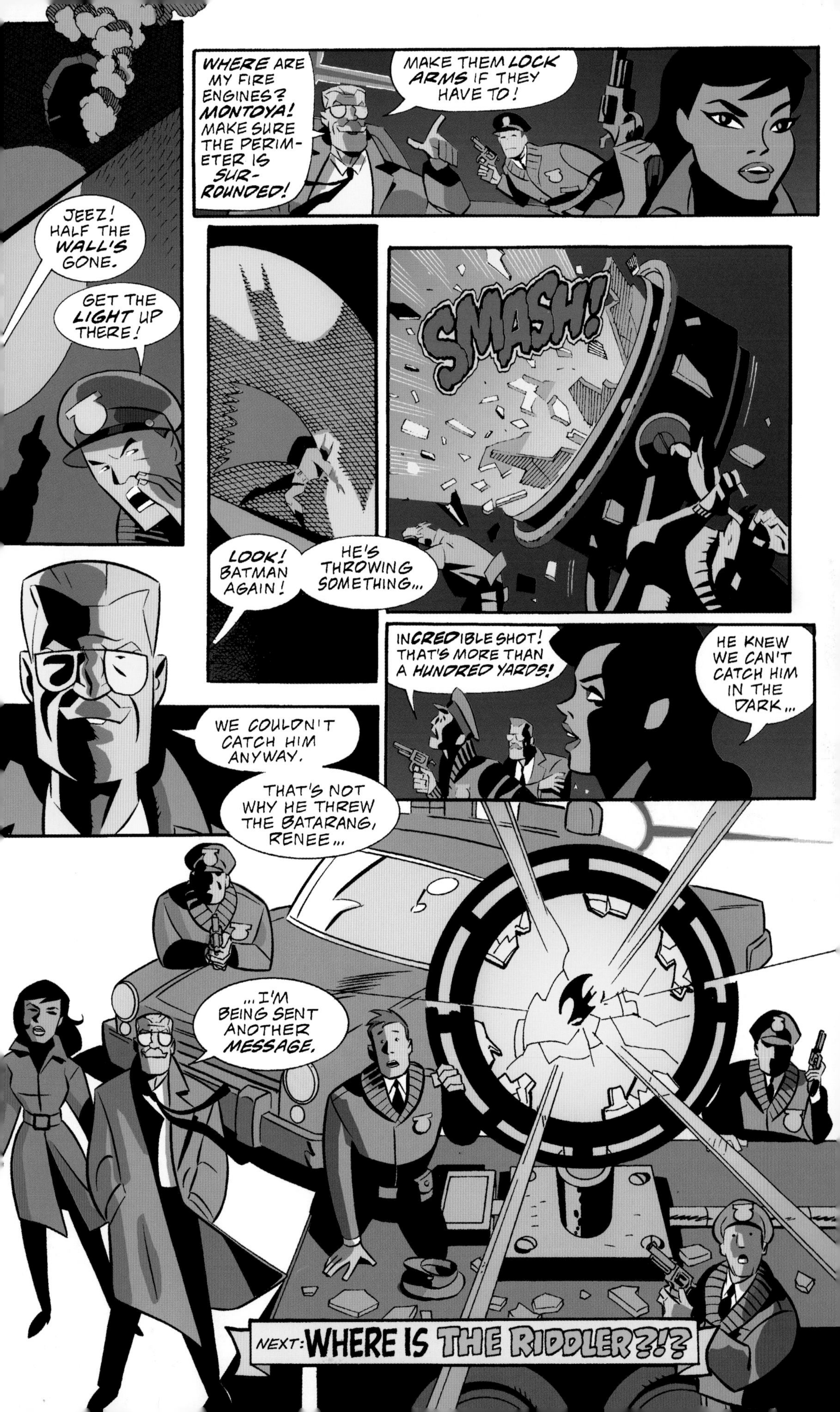

WHERE ARE MY FIRE ENGINES? MONTOYA! MAKE SURE THE PERIMETER IS SURROUNDED!
MAKE THEM LOCK ARMS IF THEY HAVE TO!
JEEZ! HALF THE WALL'S GONE.
GET THE LIGHT UP THERE!
LOOK! BATMAN AGAIN!
HE'S THROWING SOMETHING...
SMASH!
INCREDIBLE SHOT! THAT'S MORE THAN A HUNDRED YARDS!
HE KNEW WE CAN'T CATCH HIM IN THE DARK...
WE COULDN'T CATCH HIM ANYWAY.
THAT'S NOT WHY HE THREW THE BATARANG, RENEE...
...I'M BEING SENT ANOTHER MESSAGE.
NEXT: WHERE IS THE RIDDLER?!?

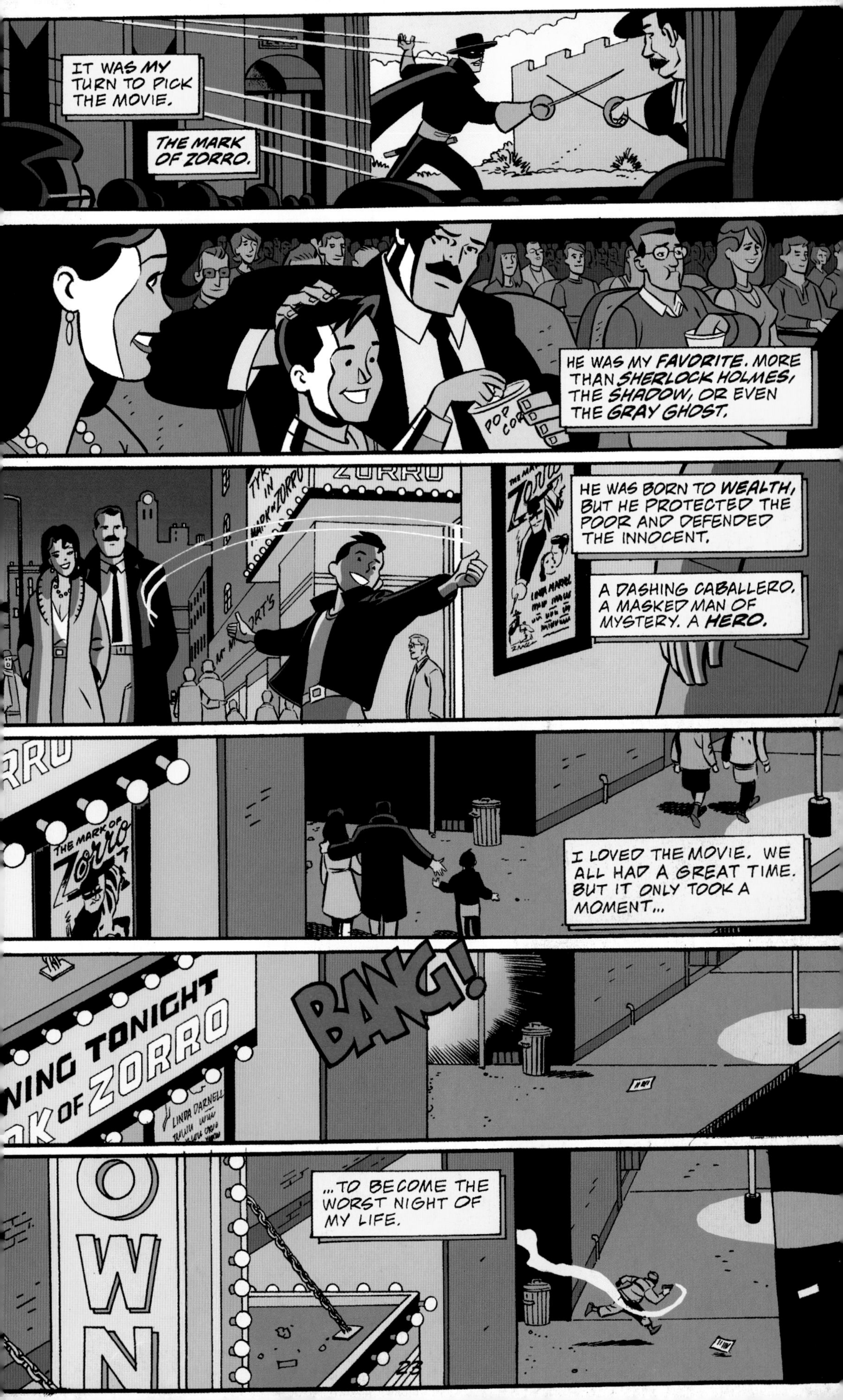

IT WAS MY TURN TO PICK THE MOVIE.
THE MARK OF ZORRO.
HE WAS MY FAVORITE. MORE THAN SHERLOCK HOLMES, THE SHADOW, OR EVEN THE GRAY GHOST.
POP COR
HE WAS BORN TO WEALTH, BUT HE PROTECTED THE POOR AND DEFENDED THE INNOCENT.
A DASHING CABALLERO, A MASKED MAN OF MYSTERY. A HERO.
ZORRO
THE MARK OF ZORRO
I LOVED THE MOVIE. WE ALL HAD A GREAT TIME. BUT IT ONLY TOOK A MOMENT...
BANG!
NING TONIGHT
K OF ZORRO
LINDA DARNELL
...TO BECOME THE WORST NIGHT OF MY LIFE.
23

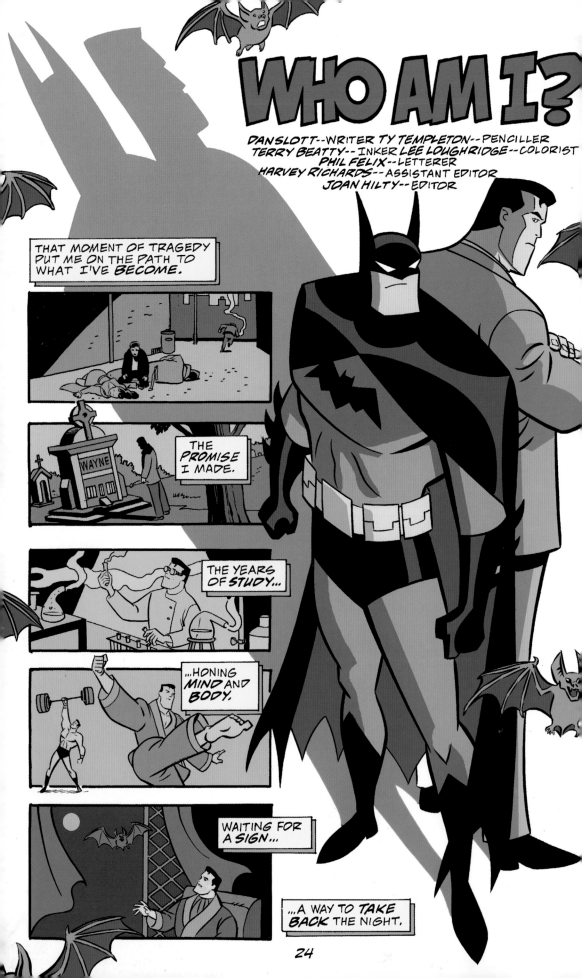

WHO AM I?

DAN SLOTT--WRITER TY TEMPLETON--PENCILLER
TERRY BEATTY--INKER LEE LOUGHRIDGE--COLORIST
PHIL FELIX--LETTERER
HARVEY RICHARDS--ASSISTANT EDITOR
JOAN HILTY--EDITOR

THAT MOMENT OF TRAGEDY PUT ME ON THE PATH TO WHAT I'VE *BECOME.*

THE *PROMISE* I MADE.

THE YEARS OF *STUDY...*

...HONING MIND AND *BODY.*

WAITING FOR A *SIGN...*

...A WAY TO TAKE BACK THE NIGHT.

24

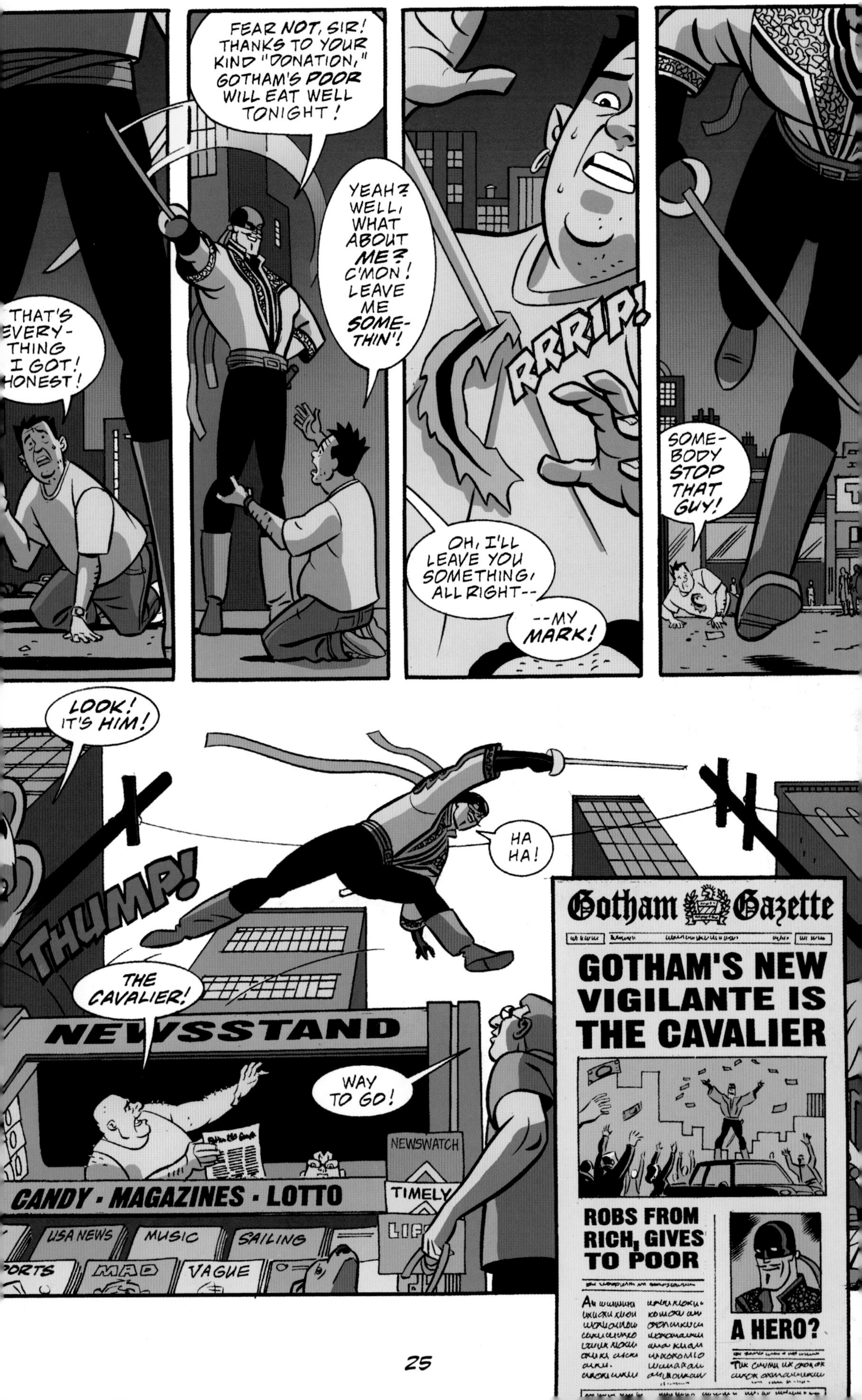
THAT'S EVERY-THING I GOT! HONEST!
FEAR NOT, SIR! THANKS TO YOUR KIND "DONATION," GOTHAM'S POOR WILL EAT WELL TONIGHT!
YEAH? WELL, WHAT ABOUT ME? C'MON! LEAVE ME SOME-THIN'!
RRRIP!
OH, I'LL LEAVE YOU SOMETHING, ALL RIGHT--
--MY MARK!
SOME-BODY STOP THAT GUY!
LOOK! IT'S HIM!
THUMP!
HA HA!
THE CAVALIER!
WAY TO GO!
NEWSSTAND
CANDY · MAGAZINES · LOTTO
NEWSWATCH
TIMELY
USA NEWS
MUSIC
SAILING
MAD
VAGUE
Gotham Gazette
GOTHAM'S NEW VIGILANTE IS THE CAVALIER
ROBS FROM RICH, GIVES TO POOR
A HERO?

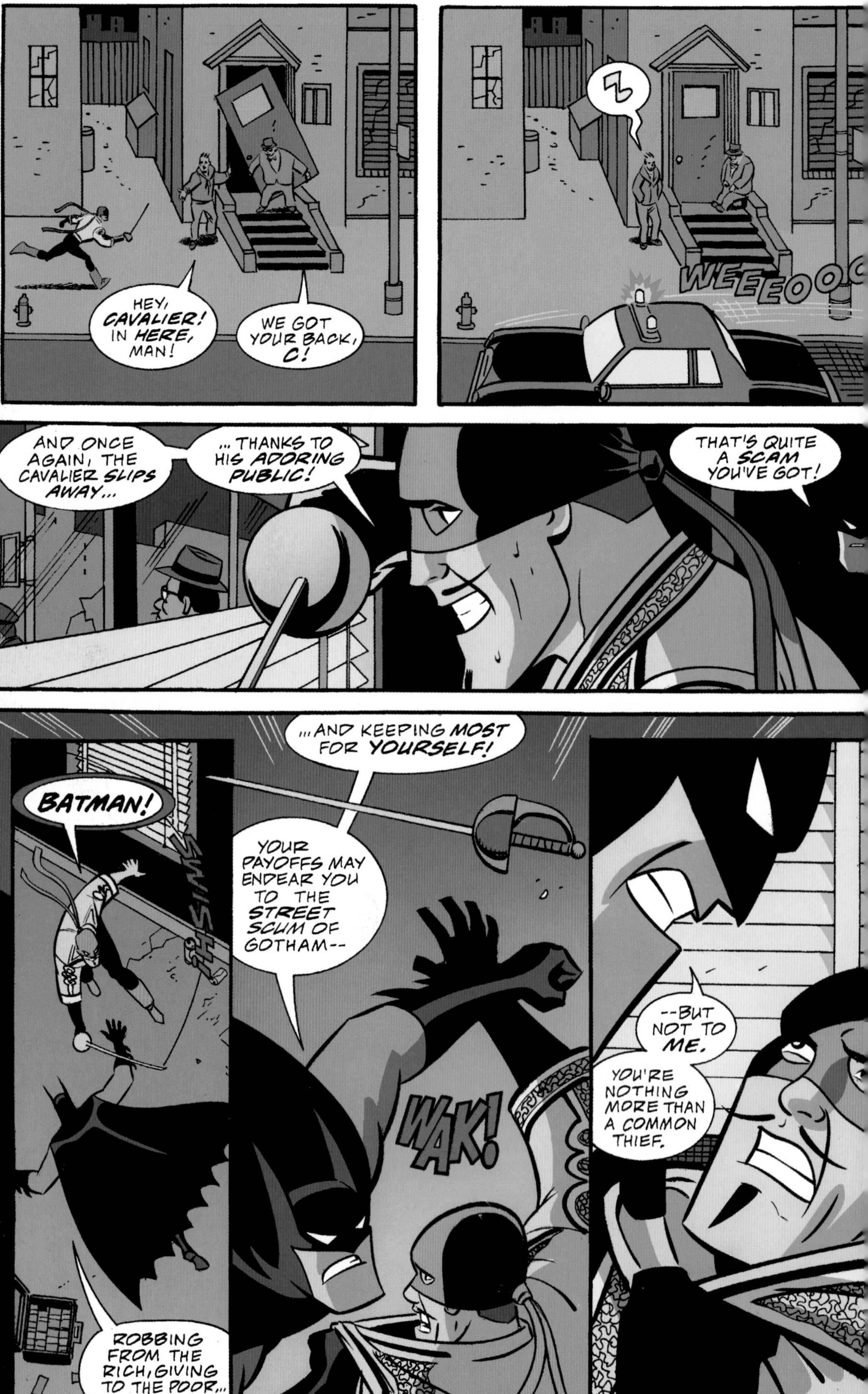
HEY, CAVALIER! IN HERE, MAN!
WE GOT YOUR BACK, C!
Z
WEEEOOO
AND ONCE AGAIN, THE CAVALIER SLIPS AWAY...
...THANKS TO HIS ADORING PUBLIC!
THAT'S QUITE A SCAM YOU'VE GOT!
BATMAN!
ROBBING FROM THE RICH, GIVING TO THE POOR...
...AND KEEPING MOST FOR YOURSELF!
YOUR PAYOFFS MAY ENDEAR YOU TO THE STREET SCUM OF GOTHAM--
WAK!
--BUT NOT TO ME.
YOU'RE NOTHING MORE THAN A COMMON THIEF.

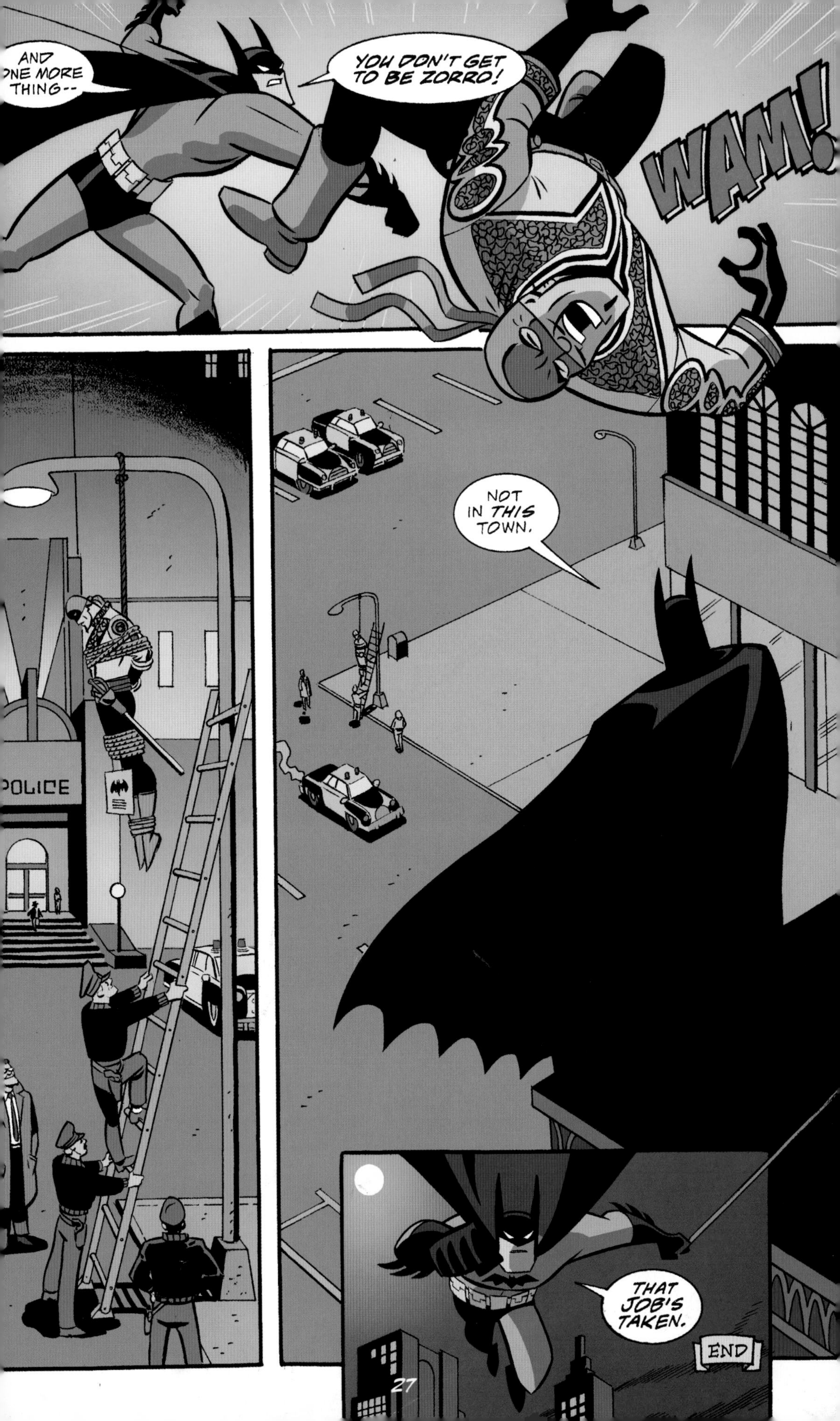

AND ONE MORE THING--
YOU DON'T GET TO BE ZORRO!
WAM!
POLICE
NOT IN THIS TOWN.
THAT JOB'S TAKEN.
END

CREATORS

TY TEMPLETON WRITER & PENCILLER

Ty Templeton was born in the wilds of downtown Toronto, Canada to a show-business family. He makes his living writing and drawing comic books, working on such characters as Batman, Superman, Spider-Man, The Simpsons, the Avengers, and many others.

DAN SLOTT WRITER

Dan Slott is a comics writer best known for his work on DC Comics' *Arkham Asylum*, and, for Marvel, *The Avengers* and the *Amazing Spider-Man*.

RICK BURCHETT PENCILLER

Rick Burchett has worked as a comics artist for more than 25 years. He has received the comics industry's Eisner Award three times, Spain's Haxtur Award, and he has been nominated for England's Eagle Award. Rick lives with his wife and two sons near St. Louis, Missouri.

TERRY BEATTY INKER

For more than ten years, Terry Beatty was the main inker of DC Comics' "animated-style" Batman comics, including *The Batman Strikes*. More recently, he worked on *Return to Perdition*, a graphic novel for DC's Vertigo Crime.

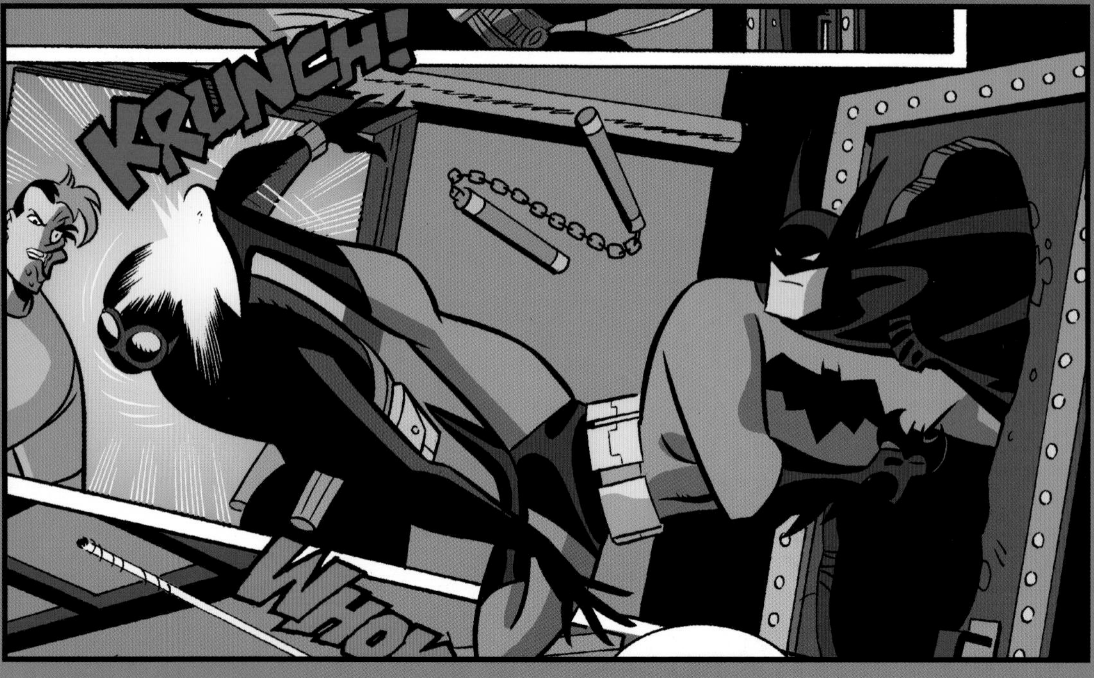
KRUNCH!

GLOSSARY

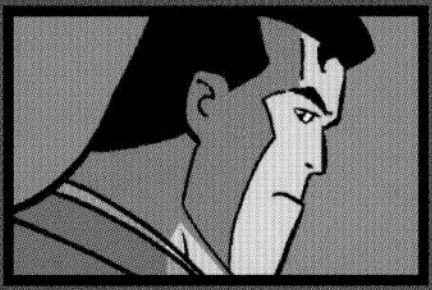

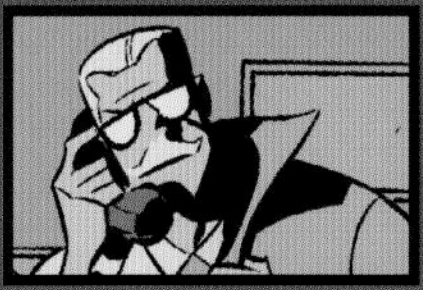

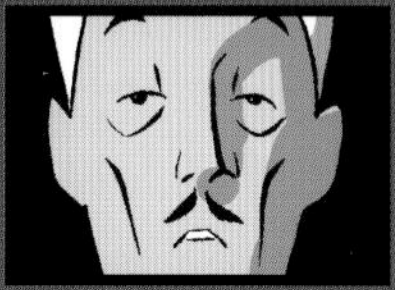

assassin (uh-SASS-uhn)--a person who kills another person, often for money

campaign (kam-PAYN)--a connected series of activities designed to bring about a particular result, such as winning an election

commissioner (kuh-MISH-uh-nur)--an official in charge of a government department, such as the police department

gruesome (GROO-suhm)--causing horror or disgust

honing (HOE-ning)--making more intense or effective

liability (lye-uh-BIL-uh-tee)--something that works as a disadvantage

neutralized (NOO-truh-lyzd)--made ineffective

outlaw (OUT-lah)--a criminal, especially one who is running away from the law

pathetic (puh-THET-ik)--causing one to feel tenderness, pity, or sorrow

perimeter (puh-RIM-uh-tur)--the boundary of an area

stealth (STELTH)--intended not to attract attention

tragedy (TRAJ-uh-dee)--a very sad event

vigilante (vij-uh-LANT-ee)--a member of a group of volunteers who decide to stop crime and punish criminals

BATMAN GLOSSARY

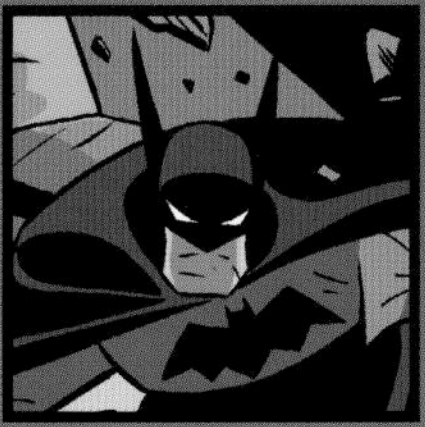

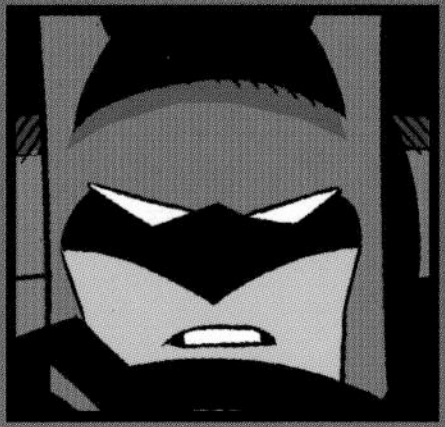

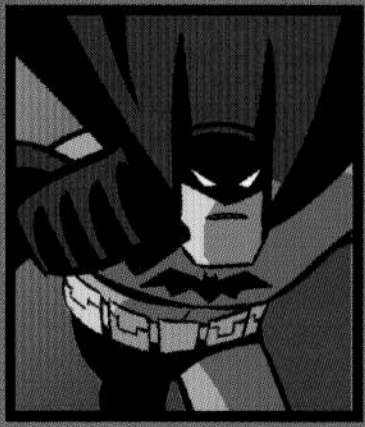

Alfred Pennyworth: Bruce Wayne's loyal butler. He knows Bruce Wayne's secret identity and helps the Dark Knight solve crimes in Gotham City.

Arkham Asylum: a psychiatric hospital in Gotham City that often holds the world's most dangerous and insane criminals, such as the Joker, Scarecrow, Two-Face, and Scarface.

Bat-Signal: a distress signal used by the Gotham City Police Department to notify the Dark Knight of danger or their need for his help.

Batarang: a metal, bat-shaped weapon that can be thrown like a boomerang.

Commissioner James Gordon: head of the Gotham City Police Department and a loyal friend of the Dark Knight.

Oswald Cobblepot: sometimes the mayor of Gotham City, but always known to Batman as the Penguin, a mastermind of the city's criminal underworld.

Society of Shadows: an organization of highly trained assassins led by Ra's al Ghul, a centuries-old assassin who hopes to rid the world of humanity.

Two-Face: after having his face disfigured, Harvey Dent, the city's former district attorney, turned to a life of crime, basing life or death decisions on the flip of a coin.

VISUAL QUESTIONS & PROMPTS

1. The way a character's eyes and mouth look, also known as their facial expression, can tell a lot about the emotions he or she is feeling. In the image at right, how do you think the Dark Knight is feeling? Use the illustration to explain your answer.

--BUT NOT TO ME.

YOU'RE NOTHING MORE THAN A COMMON THIEF.

1

2. The Dark Knight often uses high-tech devices while solving crimes, including flying weapons called Batarangs [see panel below]. Identify two other panels in which Batman uses one of his high-tech gadgets. Describe them and write about how these devices could be useful in fighting crime.

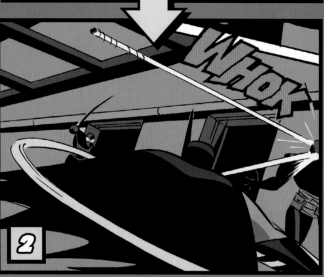

WHOK

2

3. The Dark Knight is an expert martial artist. Find at least two panels in this book where Batman uses this skill. Do you believe he could've solved those problems differently? Why or why not?

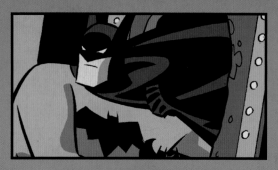

...HONING *MIND* AND *BODY.*

3

4. Several of Batman's worst enemies appear in this book, including the Joker, Scarface, Killer Croc, Poison Ivy, and Two-Face. In the panel below, why do you think Two-Face chose to help Batman instead of hurt him?

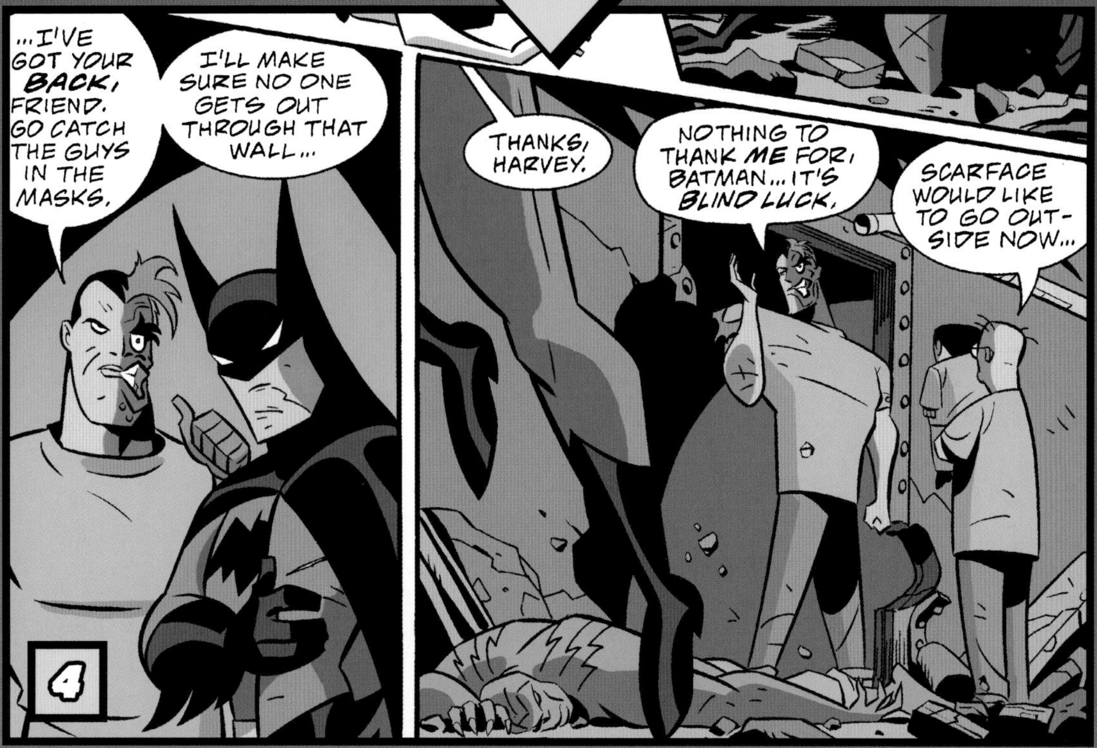
...I'VE GOT YOUR BACK, FRIEND. GO CATCH THE GUYS IN THE MASKS.
I'LL MAKE SURE NO ONE GETS OUT THROUGH THAT WALL...
THANKS, HARVEY.
NOTHING TO THANK ME FOR, BATMAN... IT'S BLIND LUCK.
SCARFACE WOULD LIKE TO GO OUT-SIDE NOW...
4

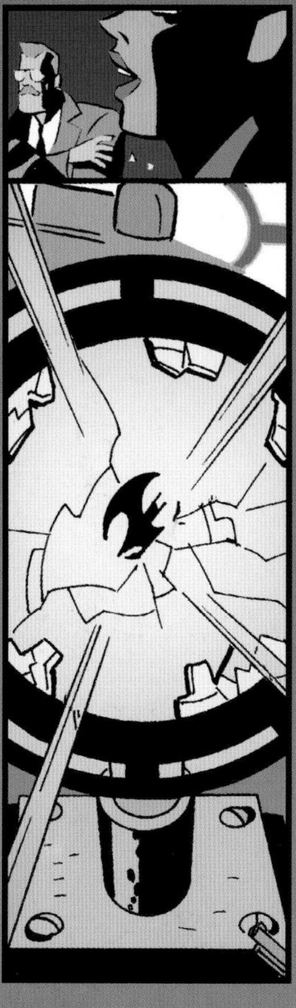

5. The Dark Knight fights to rid the city of crime. At the end of the story, why do you think Batman chose to destroy the police department's Bat-Signal? Explain your answer using examples from the story.

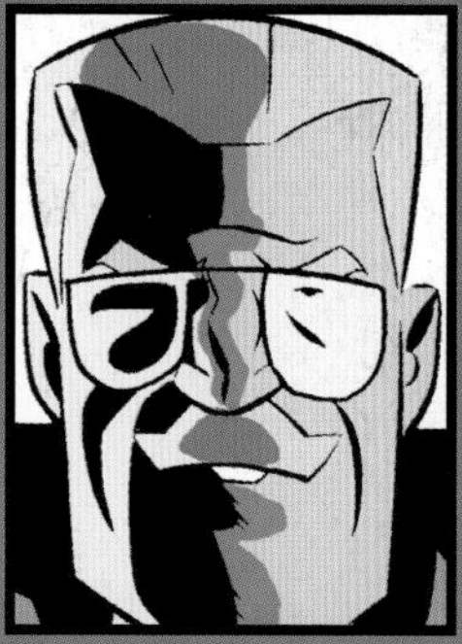

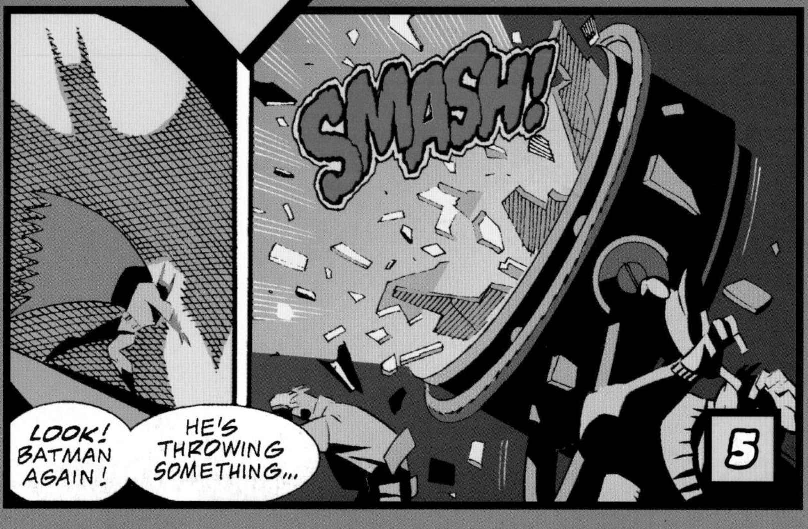
SMASH!
LOOK! BATMAN AGAIN!
HE'S THROWING SOMETHING...
5

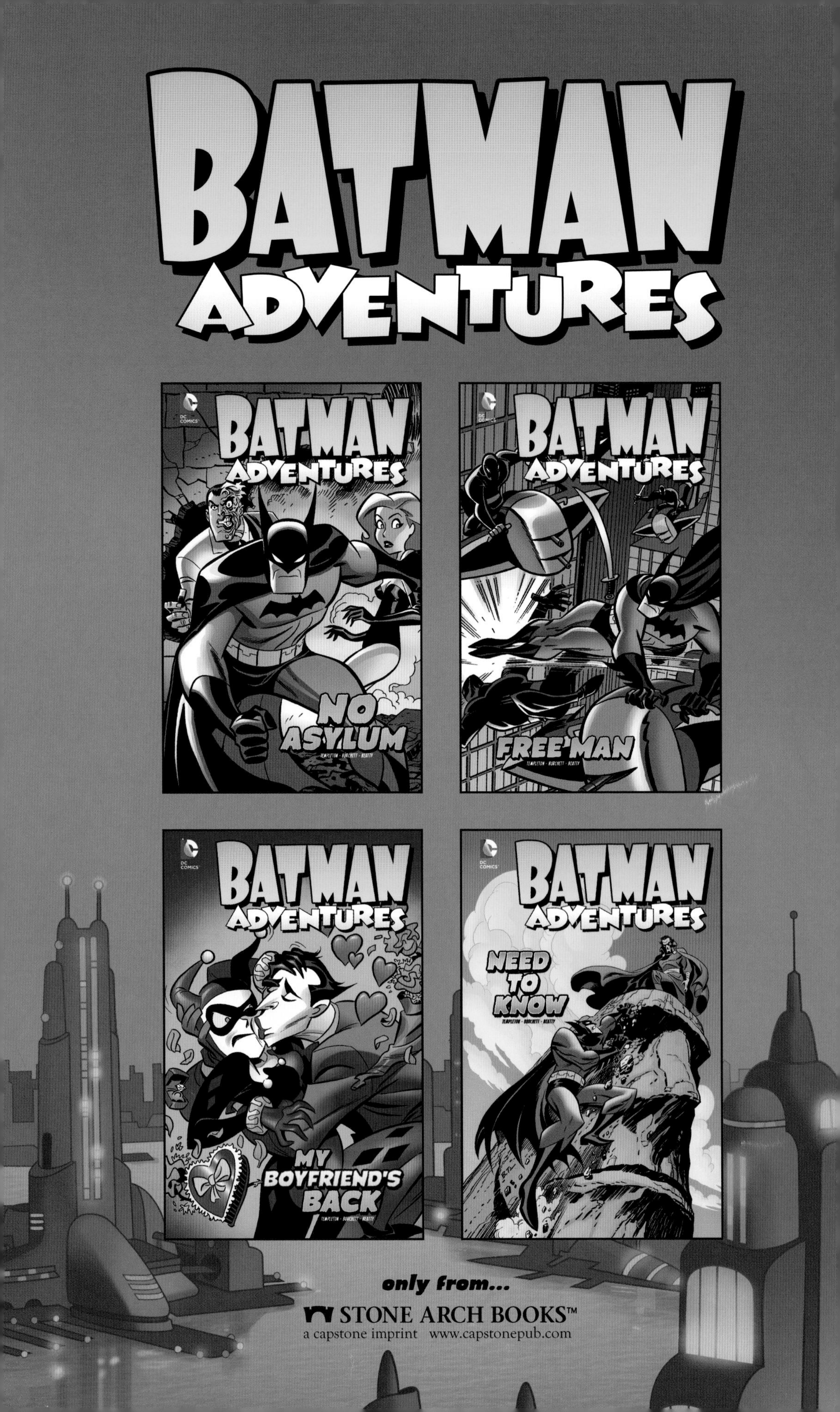
BATMAN
ADVENTURES
BATMAN ADVENTURES
NO ASYLUM
TEMPLETON · BURCHETT · BEATTY
BATMAN ADVENTURES
FREE MAN
TEMPLETON · BURCHETT · BEATTY
BATMAN ADVENTURES
MY BOYFRIEND'S BACK
TEMPLETON · BURCHETT · BEATTY
BATMAN ADVENTURES
NEED TO KNOW
TEMPLETON · BURCHETT · BEATTY
only from...
STONE ARCH BOOKS™
a capstone imprint www.capstonepub.com